Lifespan Narratives

THE GERMAN LIST

ALEXANDER KLUGE

Lifespan Narratives

TEN STORIES FROM A TIME OF DISRUPTION

CHRONICLE OF EMOTIONS, NOTEBOOK 3

TRANSLATED BY
LEILA VENNEWITZ AND ALEXANDER BOOTH

LONDON NEW YORK CALCUTTA

Seagull Books, 2025

Originally published as *Lebensläufe* in *Chronik der Gefühle, Band I*

First published in English translation by Seagull Books, 2025

ISBN 978 1 80309 491 5

British Library Cataloguing-in-Publication Data
A catalogue record for this book is available from the British Library

Typeset by Seagull Books, Calcutta, India
Printed and bound in Calcutta, India, by Hyam Enterprises

Contents

TEN LIFESPAN NARRATIVES 1

Lieutenant Boulanger 4

Demise of an Attitude 19

Fräulein von Posa 32

E. Schincke 46

Anita G. 85

Manfred Schmidt 103

Sergeant Major Hans Peickert 134

A Change of Career 151

An Experiment in Love 164

Korti 170

TEN LIFESPAN NARRATIVES

THEIR MASS OF EXPERIENCE

TRAVERSED BY THE YEAR OF WAR 1945

In the century of engineers, in 1941, during the war between Germany and Russia, **Lieutenant Boulanger** gets tangled up in a series of executions. After 1949, he sees difficulties in categorizing his behaviour, active in a completely different profession and living in a much more prudent world as he is. The cut of a sickle divides his life in two.

In the spring of 1945, during a time in which fatalities were increasing, **Chief of Detectives Scheliha** (Central Criminal Investigation Department, German Reich, Berlin) travels to West Prussia seeking information about an individual murder case. We see the murderer escaping in a carriage bound for the west at the same time as the Chief of Detectives is being led to the east, from which he will not return before 1953, as a prisoner of war.

Fräulein von Posa, a landowner. Change is coming. A small branch of a disturbed noble family. What is the meaning of bravery at a time when all that matters is not to be trampled to death?

The **classical philologist Eberhard Schincke** transports his belly (along with his knowledge of Latin) into the countryside while evacuating schoolchildren from town; he develops a fondness for a strapping young man by the name of Carlton, who dies in the chaos of war. Does self-cultivation help when you're in a pinch?

A young prisoner, **Anita G.**, serving time in a women's prison in Frankfurt on the Main; her Jewish parents hunted during the time of the Third Reich. Saved against all odds, they set up a commercial enterprise on what would later become the territory of the GDR. And were thus considered capitalists and hunted once again. Their daughter Anita G.—who, so to speak, has already got to know two fatherlands in this particular way—escapes to the Federal Republic. She steals one of her coworker's sweaters. 'Theft from a comrade,' an aggravated offence. After serving her sentence, she races through West Germany before seeking protection once again behind bars.

Cheerful **Manfred Schmidt**, a reckless chicken: the life narrative of one who got away, who was never personally in danger. A MAN WITHOUT DESTINY. 'He lets himself be burnt.' Not guiltless, if without a guilty conscience he very well may be.

Sergeant Major Hans Peickert. A 'War Profiteer'. Successfully seeks his own advantage. Helps others, too. His cleverness leads to his death.

A passionate patriot of educational reform, the **teacher Schwebkowski**, knowing that he is responsible for future generations, finds himself confronted by the 1950s' inspectorate of schools. No educational reform far and wide. When he is unable to help a friend he cares about, he changes professions.

An Experiment in Love. The guards of an extermination camp experiment on two prisoners. Is this story trying to say that at a certain level of misfortune, love can no longer be generated?

The justice system in the Third Reich is a murder-machine. Of all the organizations that lived on past 1945, it shows the most tenacious power to survive. This is the story of a district-court judge named **Korti** who belongs to that machine. 'A human being equipped with their character armour.' Korti's raison d'être is one based on self-defence and prudence. An institution that recruits such people enjoys an almost eternal life. 'Korti, endless.'

FIGURE 1
Anita G.

LIEUTENANT BOULANGER

I

In February 1942, the head of the Department of Anatomy, Reich University, Strasbourg, Professor A. Hirt, sent the following communication to one of the leading men in the Reich government:

> *Re: Securing of craniums of Jewish-Bolshevist commissars for purposes of scientific investigation at the Reich University of Strasbourg*
>
> Cranium collections are on hand representing almost every race and people. The Jews are the only group for which science has an insufficient number of craniums at its disposal in order to obtain conclusive results. The war in Eastern Europe now provides an opportunity to remedy this deficiency. Jewish-Bolshevist commissars, the embodiment of a repulsive but typical subhuman species, make it possible for us to lay hands on tangible scientific proof if we can secure their craniums.
>
> The most efficient method of acquiring and preserving this cranium material is in the form of instructions to the army to henceforth immediately hand over all Jewish-Bolshevist commissars—alive—to the military police. The military police will in turn receive special instructions to report to a specified location the number and whereabouts of these prisoners as they are delivered, and to see that they are kept under close guard pending the arrival of a specially

authorized officer. The officer charged with the securing of this material (a junior medical officer, or a medical student, attached to the army or possibly the military police, and supplied with car and driver) will take a prearranged series of photographs and anthropological measurements, and to the best of his ability establish origin, date of birth and other personal data. When the death of the Jew has subsequently been brought about, in a way that will not damage the head, the officer will separate the head from the trunk and, after immersing it in preserving fluid in a metal container (with a close-fitting lid) specially provided for the purpose, forward it to its destination. The photographs, measurements and other data pertinent to the head and eventually to the skull will permit the laboratory to embark on comparative anatomical research, as well as a study of the racial origin, pathological features of the cranium formation, brain formation and size and many additional aspects.

By virtue of its functions and objectives, the new Reich University of Strasbourg would appear to be the most suitable place for the preservation and study of the cranium material thus acquired.

A. Hirt

The Personnel Department of the army offered Lieutenant Rudolf B., of Flörsheim (on the Main), the commander of this special mission. Boulanger had been a medical student. In effect, the acceptance of this special mission meant a short cut to promotion. The prospect of a transfer to research was held out. Boulanger seized the opportunity.

II

In 1942, Rudolf B. was 34 years old. He was of medium height. His complexion was olive, his eyelids were hairless. He may have had Romans or (eighteenth-century) Frenchmen among his ancestors. He had volunteered for the engineering corps, was prepared to shine, to seize advantages, to arrive at speedy solutions. For years he found no opportunity of conquering, he did not pass his state medical examination, he had no technical qualifications. All he had were good intentions, and with those he waited for his chance, which finally came in 1942.

Good Intentions

If executing a task consists of proceeding straight along a prescribed path without flagging or allowing oneself to be impeded, it might be said that B. fulfilled such a task to the highest degree. Vigour and intelligence operated—if, like Seneca, one is to regard a human being as a marching army—in this case at the very centre of the front. In practice, however, none of B.'s activities proceeded along a straightforward course. Problems of ambiguity arose, and his determination to succeed was not enough to solve them. In cases of this kind, there is no such thing as good intentions, since good intentions are beside the point. B. decided such ambiguous cases on the basis of the greatest effectiveness.

What He Would Rather Have Been

Since boyhood, B. had wanted to be a hydraulic engineer. However, there was no school of hydraulic engineering near Flörsheim (on the Main). After his graduation, therefore, Boulanger decided to study medicine in Frankfurt (on the Main). Difficulty in passing the state examination put an end to his studies. B. was drafted into the army.

Advantages of His New Post

On taking over his special mission, Boulanger became eligible for a front-line allowance of Reichsmark 2.65 per day. Lieutenant Boulanger was responsible for the allotting of duties, more particularly: the hours of duty. Later, he sometimes took advantage of this to make a brief excursion to some place of interest in Russia. Furthermore, there was the possibility of being invited to various staff headquarters where one could make lifelong friendships. Three: there was the chance of procuring extra blankets, supplies and rations at various commissariats, a relatively easy matter for a mobile outfit such as B.'s special detachment. Finally, there was no overlooking the fact that the connection with the academic world, even if only as an agent, had advantages of a prestige nature.

Superiority of the Academic World

A connection with the academic world means lifelong security. The academic world is free. The members of the academic world rank immediately behind party members; at social functions, they come after the SS but before the German East Africans.

Chain of Command

In disciplinary matters, B. in his new post came under the command of the Personnel Department as represented by the Army Group Chiefs, who were in turn represented by the senior Army Corps General commanding the odd-numbered Army Corps. B. had no dealings with any of the senior army judges. In fact, the only superior who could give him orders was the academic world. In a formal sense, B. also came under the jurisdiction of the divisional commander of whatever sector of the front he happened to be in. If necessary, B. could absent himself from their jurisdiction by moving to a different divisional area. But no conflicts arose.

Relationship to an Officer's Honour

At times, during the years following 1942, B. found his butcher's duties—which other officers compared to a hangman's job—abhorrent. Some officers entrusted with this task might have taken to drink. While working on his first case, B. had to overcome mental inhibitions. In that particular instance, B. deserted his post just as the head was being severed, thus incurring the risk of his assistants making mistakes. B.' s thought: You must not take to drink now.

On the other hand, there are no genuine inhibitions involved in killing someone else if one can see clearly enough that it is not one's own death that is taking place. B.' s sense of insecurity during much of the procedure was based mainly on the disapproval of his activities by various officers with whom he was friendly. But this disapproval was not valid. When B. later rejected one or another of the commissars delivered to him by the army, these same officers, who criticized his special mission, were in command of the firing squad executing the commissar (which usually resulted in mutilating the head).

Relations with Women

Excellent.

Prison Life

For many men, the conquest of Eastern Europe meant a removal of barriers after years of conforming to a narrow way of life. Hence the occupation should, by rights, have brought with it rape and pillage, or at least an adequate number of brothels. Instead, the occupation was carried out according to regulations that might just as well have been those of a prison administration. In this respect, the great liberation of Eastern Europe in 1941 and the following years coincided for B. with the greatest disappointment of his life.

Initial Visit to Professor Hirt

Luncheon at Professor Hirt's consisted of four courses: chicken bisque, fish, saddle of venison, macédoine of fruits. The professor's nieces had been invited for coffee. It was late afternoon by the time Boulanger took leave. He could almost have fallen in love with one of the nieces. Next morning, he boarded his eastbound train.

Activities started in the region of Orel. Not everyone handed over to Boulanger was a commissar. It turned out that the number of commissars was exaggerated, and the classifying of commissars as 'Jewish-Bolshevist' was arbitrary. Most of them were simply partisan leaders casually classified as commissars. While the army showed great reluctance to deliver officers taken prisoner at the front, it was most liberal in handing over partisans, although experience showed that commissars were more likely to be found among the officers. However, the army officers did take back partisans when required (and then shot them themselves), exchanging them for captured front commissars whom they handed over to the military police.

The main problem consisted of the proper classification of the prisoners as commissars, and of the use of the additional criterion 'Jewish-Bolshevist'. Not every Jewish-Russian officer came into this category, nor did every Bolshevik. Boulanger tried to obtain data on the question: With what rank in the party hierarchy does an officer become a commissar? From several staff officers whom he questioned, he received inconclusive data that only served to convince him even further of the arbitrariness of the selection methods. The care he devoted to the execution of his special mission, and the extra research he put into the clarifying of its basic principles, was at par with the care which otherwise in the army would have only been expended on the awarding of the highest decorations. At some headquarters, this earned B.'s unit the title of

'Decorations Detachment'. Even a negatively evaluated mission—in fact, especially such a mission—must be accomplished with all the energy and intelligence at one's command. In so doing, one must compensate for what has not been thoroughly thought out or is subject to criticism in the original definition of one's duties. Despite his efforts, Boulanger knew he could not avoid making any number of errors, and that these were sometimes to the prisoners' advantage and sometimes not. The errors in favour of Russians (e.g. those who were not classified as Jews although they were) could be compensated for by safety margins, a procedure not permissible in the case of the erroneous inclusion of innocent persons (e.g. Jews who were not commissars, commissars who were not Jews), since in such cases a safety margin, while it reduced the probability of error, jeopardized the effectiveness of the method. In practice, the only way to determine racial origin was by such primitive factors as appearance, family and first names, or perhaps skull measurements. The strong possibility of error made it seem advisable to discontinue the mission altogether. By the same token, it followed that, if the mission were continued, the errors must be tolerated and allowed for in the calculations. So Boulanger was beset by endless doubts at the same time as he felt that the doubts must not be permitted to hamper the careful and conscientious execution of his mission. It was therefore important to him to convey his ideas and good intentions to an area where they could not harm the performance of his duties: during this period, he read philosophical works, for he was toying with the idea of later extending his (previously abandoned) studies in this subject.

III

The task of bringing precision into the hopeless end of the captured commissars completely occupied B. during the summer and winter of 1942 in the areas of the Central and Southern Army Groups (later, of the two Southern Army Groups). In February 1943, his sphere of activity was limited to the Central Army Group. At that time, Boulanger no longer restricted himself to a superficial anthropological examination nor to obtaining personal data before having the prisoners killed; he now had informal talks with the commissars in order to retain an impression not only of their external appearance but also of their minds. The body of thought thus committed to paper immediately before the writers' death served, B. believed, as additional research material; this sense of quality enhanced B.'s respect for the mission entrusted to him. It is probably always true that, to a certain extent, one identifies oneself with the enemy one kills (prior thereto one has just seen him alive). Thus Boulanger identified himself, as it were, with the intellectual achievements of his object of study. He did not know what his attitude should be when he was conscious of such feelings. Perhaps B. could, while conforming to his orders, have adapted his method to his feelings by continually extending the respite accorded the prisoners to make their written statements; but since his feelings had not the degree of clarity evinced by his former methods, he kept to his former methods.

In the summer of 1943, a further difficulty arose: the problem of increasing numbers. First, the Central Army Group retreated from the Orel bulge. The prisoner-of-war camps situated behind the front had to be hurriedly evacuated. This in turn necessitated an accelerated screening in those camps on the part of Boulanger's detachment. At times, the decision as to whether or not a case in point was a Jewish-Bolshevist commissar had to be delegated. This meant that the depots sometimes received heads and descriptions where obvious mistakes had been made. Any change in the procedure would presumably have increased this confusion.

During the late summer of 1943, the Russians took advantage of the gap forming between the southern and central German fronts (a gap which the High Command was bending every effort to close) by attacking at an entirely different point. On the day of the offensive, a crisis developed in the Second Army. The base units and the prisoner-of-war camps were caught up in the retreat. The 33rd Panzer Division brought up as a reinforcement found itself involved in the offensive while it was still aboard the trains. Desperate staffs tried to stem the retreat by maintaining their old headquarters. At that time, Boulanger's detachment, which was taking along six Russian officers, found itself near the junction of Schlichta, not far from Smolensk. Close to a wooded area, Boulanger's assistants were attacked by partisans. Boulanger himself was wounded but escaped with the vehicles in the van of the convoy. It was later assumed by the Russians that the leader of the 'Decorations Detachment' was among those captured by the partisans.

The experience was a shock to Boulanger. Surrounded by victorious German troops, by staffs which raised no objections and in the service of scientific research, there is no sense of guilt; suddenly the situation changes: like a draft springing up, a sense of guilt arises from which one must protect oneself, just as in early spring one has to be careful of open doors, for these only bring colds or even pneumonia.

IV

Boulanger spent the last days of 1943 and part of 1944 at Wiesbaden Area Military Hospital. The collapse of the Central Army Group in August 1944 dashed B.' s hopes of promotion. A transfer to Research was also out of the question. A transfer to civilian research, which would have been possible on Prof. A. Hirt's recom-mendation, was not feasible because of B.' s complete recovery. Military research was concentrating on special problems, to which Boulanger's Eastern European experience had nothing to contribute. Instead, after his recovery, he was transferred to 'Central Administration: Austrian Prisoner-of-War Camps'.

One more opportunity for total dedication presented itself to Boulanger before the end of the war, in Vienna. In January 1945, the doomed city, like a shrine, attracted troops and officers within its walls—if one can speak here of walls to be defended rather than, perhaps more properly, palaces, canals and hills. On 14 January, General Rendulic took over the defence of the city and had a thousand soldiers strung up. On 18 January (24 hours later, an air raid destroyed the opera house), the young Party Area Chief's augmented staff, which included Boulanger, attended a performance of *Lohengrin*. The night of 21–22 January, after two days of quiet, the Russians embarked on a new major assault on Vienna. Within a few hours, the opportunity of meeting death here was exhausted. Russian tanks were lined up on the northern bank of the canal; practically speaking, the city was in Russian hands. All that remained of the last great chance was the biological factor, pure and simple. B. managed to reach the American lines. There he gave himself up.

V

How Do People Like B. Live Today?

In the summer of 1961, reporters tracked Boulanger down as a packer in a paper mill near Cologne. His offences were subject to statutory limitations. A correspondent from *L'Humanité* asked for an interview. B. was ushered into the board room and answered questions. When asked about his present beliefs, he replied that he was a Marxist. What was he doing? There was nothing one could do.

Contagion from the Enemy

He said he had been infected, as it were, by his enemies, since naturally he had talked to some of the prisoners. Did that mean he thought the imperialists in the German Federal Republic were in particular danger of becoming Communists? Of course not. One would have to be in closer contact with the enemy. Chop off his head? In a sense, yes. That was carrying the Christian spirit too far, said the reporter from *L'Humanité*.

Renewed Encounter with the Academic World

The war over, there was a chance of resuming his studies as soon as the universities reopened. He was given credit for four pre-war semesters.

Expiation and Surrogate

QUESTION. I see by your forehead that you joined a students' duelling club?

ANSWER. That was another compromise.

QUESTION. But how did you land in jail?

ANSWER. After a row with the principal of the institute at Marburg in 1953, I tried to start up in business on my own, in the textile branch. This fresh start ended in disaster, that's to say, I had trouble making payments and so they put me in jail.

QUESTION. With criminals?

ANSWER. They don't make any distinction.

QUESTION. How many years?

ANSWER. Three. The prison padre regarded it as an expiation for my deeds during the war.

QUESTION. You mean he forgave you because they were commissars?

ANSWER. In his eyes, the prison sentence made everything all right. He thought I might go and look after lepers in Ethiopia.

QUESTION. What kind of a job would that be?

ANSWER. You get leprosy, too, but in return you can save the lives of a few lepers.

QUESTION. Not a very fair deal, to exchange about 60 to 100 well-trained key men for five or six lepers saved in Ethiopia. For that, you would have to believe that all men are equal.

ANSWER. I agree absolutely. Of course it's not a sensible exchange.

QUESTION. Then, if I understand you correctly, you are now carrying on the existences of the men you murdered?

ANSWER. No.

QUESTION. What are you doing in a positive sense?

ANSWER. I've already told you: one's not allowed to do anything. Just have a conviction.

QUESTION. That's something!

ANSWER. But the change in me is not meant either as expiation or surrogate.

How the 'Decorations' Method Worked

We usually arrived in the evening, because in the morning we were busy somewhere else, with dissecting, embalming, etc., and sometimes we covered considerable distances during the day—our day began at 5 a.m. and was never over before midnight; towards evening, we would reach a depot, arriving in our jeeps with trailers carrying the instruments and other materials. Sometimes there were headquarters near by, and we would be invited for a bite to eat or a drink, but often they would ignore us, especially during our first visit to the boundary-sector divisions of the Northern Army Group, which were not actually part of our territory. It was almost as if the climate had something to do with it: you might say that, going from north to south, there was a greater acceptance of our mission, i.e. in the south more, in the north less. The reasons had nothing to do with climate: in the Northern Army Group, which had been almost stationary since the winter of 1941 the peacetime influence among the top brass had remained more constant, in other words: the atmosphere was conservative; it was different in the southern and central areas, where fresh recruits were continually injecting new ideas. There, we were not regarded with the same scepticism. I must say, though, that even among the conservative forces, there was no actual disapproval of our work, they just made it clear that they were dubious about our methods. They would have preferred us to shoot the commissars according to military regulations instead of killing them by injection, which we did so as to keep the heads intact. Execution by shooting was the very thing that would have destroyed the heads, and it was the heads that were vital to us.

You are wandering from the subject. What was your procedure?

First, we looked at the takings of that particular day. Most of those who were supposed to be commissars were not. In one case it would be a noncom, in another an anti-aircraft officer. Anyone who was too outspoken in camp and harangued his men gave the impression of behaving like a commissar. From time to time, you would hear the expression 'Freemason' commissar. Although it was probably contrary to my orders and meant that, later, when I had to carry out the rest of the job, I had the added burden of personal feelings, I frequently had talks with the prisoners, since in my experience this was the best method of selection. The level of education or training gave the best indication of which ones might be commissars. Where there was a certain level of intellectual superiority, there was every probability that he was a commissar.

I don't want to bore you with the finer points of our method. When the selection was made, we took the Jewish-Bolshevist commissars to be measured, this was seldom done the same night, often it wasn't until the next morning, because, after the lengthy selection procedure, we would be dead beat by the time we returned to our quarters. To save on guard personnel, we often took the commissars back to our quarters with us, and this laid us open to the accusation of abusing them homosexually. No such case is known to me. One thing is certain: not even a love affair of this kind could have saved any of the commissars at this stage of proceedings. The local troops were responsible for the bodies we left behind.

Caution

In future, he would refuse to be put in charge of such work or any work like it. He would be extremely careful. And if others did it and he looked on? Caution should be used there too; probably he would do nothing and await developments.

Activity and Inactivity

The 'Decorations Detachment' was his attempt at activity in his life, and the counterpart to it was now inactivity, so that it was even possible to say: I am a Marxist; but there is nothing one can do.

Road Closed to the East

QUESTION. Why don't you go to eastern Germany?

ANSWER. They disregard statutory limitations there.

What Happened to Professor A. Hirt?

That's a good question. In 1944, when I was in Vienna, I got a postcard from Professor Hirt. In Strasbourg, the Allies came across the remains of his skull collection—there had not been time to destroy it completely. The Foreign Office asked him for an official reaction to the accusation raised in Swiss newspapers; on 6 April 1945, Hirt promised a prompt reply. Later, he disappeared.

Did He Have Any After Effects from His 1943 Wound?

Pain in his right elbow, a periodically recurring inflammation of the ligaments: whenever that cropped up, he went to a chiropractor for treatment.

No Coffee

During the interview, a human relationship had developed between B. and the reporter from *L'Humanité*. When the interview was over, they would have liked to have a cup of coffee together. But that turned out to be impossible: coffee was not served in the canteen at that hour, so as to not give the staff an excuse to leave their jobs. And in the canteen no one was allowed to sit down. So B. and the interviewer parted without having a cup of coffee.

DEMISE OF AN ATTITUDE

Chief of Detectives Scheliha

I

In January 1945, Chief of Detectives Scheliha, Central Criminal Investigation Department of the German Reich, travelled on official business to the Elbing area. This is what had happened: since November 1944, a landowner by the name of von Z. had been under investigation by the local police in connection with a murder. For various reasons, however, no charges had been made. In these final months of the war, the authorities were reluctant to take drastic steps against a person enjoying powerful connections. Many local authorities, as well as some senior officials in Elbing, were more inclined to send the suspect to the front. But before proceedings could be terminated in this manner, the files found their way to the Central Criminal Investigation Department in Berlin. Chief of Detectives Scheliha was instructed to clear up the matter on the spot.

Chief of Detectives Scheliha requested the services of two inspectors, two assistants, a stenographer and a small police detachment; these were to go on ahead at night by automobile, taking the Fürstenwalde-Schwiebus road. It was his intention to combine the investigation of this case with one last inspection of West Prussia, before that province was also overrun by Russian troops. He followed the advance party by taking the day train to Elbing. That day, General Hossbach's troops abandoned the Lötzen barrier and, as a kind of roving pocket, broke through the Russian lines to the west, the Russians having already moved in behind these troops and begun to occupy the province of East Prussia.

It was really a mystery why the local National Socialist government officials did not see to it that the suspect received the punishment he deserved.

II

Scheliha did not remain in the fortified town of Elbing, where the jails were in the process of being emptied and many bands of traitors and deserters were being shot; instead, he left an inspector behind him, with instructions to keep him posted on the circumstances surrounding the murder and the numerous rumours circulating about events at the front. At the district jail outside Elbing, he was informed that, in connection with some local disturbances on the part of foreign workers, there had been a successful prison break. One of the prisoners had been Z., who was being held for questioning. Late that day, Scheliha and his staff were driven to Z.'s estate not far from Elbing. He could not understand why this man had not been more strictly guarded.

As could have been foreseen, the suspect was no longer to be found on the estate. Scheliha had some of the farm hands questioned, as well as the priest and the party leader from the next village. It was established that the suspect was spotted on the grounds for a few hours but had then continued his flight in a hunting brake, taking six horses with him (so as to always have two for relief). Scheliha assumed the suspect would avoid heading due west in the direction of Pomerania or Lower Silesia; he judged that the danger of falling into the hands of military police and being taken for a deserter would outweigh any advantage offered by that shorter route. More likely, the suspect had fled in a south-easterly curve towards the front, for that way he had some hope of reaching what had once been Poland (now known as the General Government). The collapse of the Vistula front and the rapid thrust of the Russian armies had created such confusion that the suspect could risk approaching the frontier of the German Reich from that side. Incidentally, at the time the crime was committed, there had not been a single foreign workers' camp anywhere in the vicinity of the estate, nor a single foreign worker, loiterer or deserter who could have committed the crime. Allusions to roaming foreigners occurred in the statements of every defendant pleading not guilty. Scheliha's attitude to this kind of excuse was basically a sceptical one. He did, however, investigate the possibility of some person other than the suspect having committed the crime. The farm hands were housed in barracks; during working hours, they were watched. They had no access to the manor house, the scene of the murder. The information gathered by the inspector left behind at Elbing relating to the background of the Z. murder was communicated by telephone: no specific protection for Z. was apparent, but there was a widespread disinclination to concentrate on this murder at the present time. Party officials had not been consulted. Legal opinion held, among other things, that at the moment the real danger emanated not from people like von Z. but from countless rebellious and desperate bands of individuals who now, towards the end of the war and with the breakthrough on the Vistula front, saw their chance to revolt. The District Attorney's office likewise took the attitude that in this tense and precarious situation one had no right to kill off one's own countrymen, so to speak; the case must be regarded from the point of view of its consequences. None of these views corresponded to Chief of Detectives Scheliha's opinion.

III

Scheliha needed less than an hour to convince himself of the landowner's guilt. He gave orders for the situation in which the corpse had been found to be outlined in chalk on the floor, and then, with the aid of his assistants, he re-enacted the rather crude crime. One of the labourers was found to be in possession of articles of Z.'s clothing which, as was to be expected, revealed traces of blood. These and other items of evidence were sent to Elbing on a farm cart. Even the awkward fact that the murder had been a particularly brutal one and hence was difficult to ascribe to an educated person of good family (which prompted the thought that perhaps a foreign worker was responsible after all) was satisfactorily explained on the basis of the statements made regarding the personality of the suspect. Actually, the suspect—and all those interrogated concurred in this—was a man of high moral standards which, in this instance, had first to be overcome. It was obvious that the mutilation of the guest's head was attributable to the exceptional demands which the landowner normally made of his conscience. It had been an explosion, as it were, of this conscience which, under these particular circumstances, was unable to prevent the crime and thus sought a different outlet in mutilation.

Scheliha left his second inspector behind on the estate with instructions to continue the necessary interrogations until the Russians approached, and then, as the danger increased, to make for Berlin via the fortified town of Elbing. He himself set off by car with his two assistants and the stenographer—to whom en route he dictated a detailed report on information received to date—for the railway junction of Schmielau. From there he hoped to quickly travel south by train or handcar, and possibly intercept the murderer on one of the routes leading south. However, some 30 kilometres before Schmielau, he encountered a triple column of military vehicles. Trucks, three abreast, were driving along the relatively narrow highway; further on were armoured cars, two abreast, soldiers clinging to the sides of the vehicles. These columns were trying to rcach thc fortified town of Elbing, and thus pushed all oncoming traffic—including the Chief of Detectives' vehicles—off the highway. Some dispatch riders, following instructions, were clearing the way or the column, which otherwise would have cleared a way for itself; they referred the Chief of Detectives to the next officer. But it was a long time before a senior officer could be found, as it was by no means easy to communicate with an officer in that rapidly moving column and persuade him to dismount. The officer was in danger: if he got off, of losing his unit; he risked his life by jumping off—if he was caught away from his unit, he was likely to be court-martialled. Scheliha was therefore only able to exchange a few words with the officer before the latter jumped back up onto another truck. Scheliha ended up losing several hours during which he could do nothing but wait and hope. Even by taking advantage of the rail connections, there was no prospect of apprehending the murderer before he crossed the frontier into Poland.

IV

At the railway junction and fortified town of Schmielau, a garrison town of some 15,000 inhabitants, Chief of Detectives Scheliha found the teletype equipment of the Area Command still intact. He telephoned the inspector whom he had left behind on the suspect's estate and was given the latest results. The murder weapon had been found in the cellars of the manor house, taken to Elbing and examined there for clues. In addition, there were statements from farm hands and local inhabitants.

Via the teletype, Scheliha was able to reach a few towns and bases in East Prussia, West Prussia and the General Government (by this time it could already be called the former General Government). Thus he tried to close in on the murderer who was in the process of escaping somewhere in the nearby woods and fields; in other words, he was improvising a search, even if the method of searching contained considerable gaps. But the demands Scheliha made via the teletype met with indifference, in some cases outright refusal. Under present conditions, the search for a single individual was deemed by the local police to be impossible and unwarranted. As if this was a crime of honour! Scheliha sent the following teletype message to the chief of police in Krakow:

SCHELIHA. In the murder case (then came reference number and additional details), I am encountering obstructionist behaviour on the part of the following authorities (there followed a list of authorities). I request that these departments receive appropriate instructions. Scheliha, Chief of Detectives.

REPLY. The following departments have received instructions (names of departments followed), remaining departments listed by you can no longer be contacted. The Russians have reached Plock. Instructions given here for continuation of search. Shall we send transportation for you? Reply requested. Schulze, Commissioner-General.

SCHELIHA. Much obliged. Kindest regards.

REPLY. Kind regards.

Scheliha assumed that von Z. would try to reach the German frontier somewhere along the road between Schmielau, Klopau, and Mielczic, the whole section apparently being inadequately patrolled. To get there he would have to reach the Klopau-Mielczic road. Scheliha abandoned the idea of following up the arrest with an inspection of West Prussia. He set off in two cars in the direction of Klopau, accompanied by two assistants, a stenographer and two police officers.

V

Past a variety of crude scenes of deserters being shot along highways on which the Chief of Detectives' vehicles were unable to display their power to much advantage: on the one hand, it seemed that, in the general confusion, one murder more or less was relatively unimportant. Besides, it was difficult, if not impossible, to pick out this particular murderer among the hordes moving about in various directions; on the other hand, Scheliha could see no valid excuse for discontinuing the pursuit. He realized that the police—despite the Reich Criminal Investigation Department's excellent and up-to-date organization—were neither in a position nor empowered to cope with such a disastrous state of affairs by police methods, let alone deal successfully with it. They would have had to seize power and erect a virtual police dictatorship side by side with the existing one. All the greater, however, is a police officer's responsibility at the very moment when he is aware that the organization to which he belongs is crumbling to make every effort to carry out his duty and thus, by striving for the utmost police effectiveness, to satisfy—by intent if not in fact—the demands of violated justice.

That day, Generals Hossbach and Reinhardt, who were in command of the roving pockets in East Prussia, were dismissed and replaced by Generals Schwiethelm and von Müller. In the General Government, two field marshals attempted to rally the fleeing German troops at various points. Colonel-General Rendulic, transferred from the defence of Vienna, commandeered a villa for his headquarters and had a palisade built around it. Chief of Detectives Scheliha got as far as the environs of Klopau in his pursuit of the murderer.

VI

The following day, the situation in the Plock area deteriorated, Russian troops overran a number of roads leading from north to south more or less parallel to the Vistula. Scheliha decided to dispatch one of his vehicles, with one assistant and the stenographer, in the direction of the German frontier in order not to expose the woman unnecessarily to what might be a dangerous situation close to the front. He himself continued the pursuit towards the south. He had reason to believe he could intercept the hunting brake at an estate near Klopau. Scheliha passed through Klopau (which was surrounded shortly afterward by Russian assault troops) as an appendage to a military transport under the command of a determined lieutenant.

The day after that, in the midst of a traffic jam stretching for many miles, Scheliha was taken prisoner by Russian Guard troops not far from Klopau. He was separated from the police officers and his assistant; after being held for several days, he and a large number of other prisoners were loaded into boxcars. The files on the Z. case were destroyed when, for reasons which never became clear, the Chief of Detectives' automobile burst into flames during the brief skirmish preceding the capture.

After a hurried visit to the estate of some friends, the murderer Z. had taken—since everything pointed to the Russians not being far off—a secondary road to the west, just beyond the town of Klopau, which appeared passable for his hunting brake. A few days later, following this route, he reached the Reich frontier at Grünberg, Silesia, that part of the frontier being unguarded at the time. Via Glogau, Kottbus and Guben, and after abandoning his hunting brake, he managed to get to Schleswig-Holstein, where he was given shelter in the manor house of a large estate. He later moved to the Rhineland and settled there.

Meanwhile, Scheliha was travelling in the opposite direction.

Quotation from Kant

> 'Even if a bourgeois society should dissolve, with the consent of all its members (e.g. an island-dwelling people should decide to go their separate ways and disperse throughout the world), the last murderer still being held in prison would have first to be executed, in order for each person to receive his just deserts and for the blood-guilt not to attach to the people which has neglected to insist on this punishment; because the people may be considered as participating in this public violation of justice. It is better that one man should die than that a whole people be dragged down; for when justice perishes, the continued existence of human beings on earth becomes valueless.'

VII

By the time Scheliha returned from prison camp in 1953, circumstances in Germany had changed. Scheliha refrained from any further pursuit of Z., who now occupied a position in the Rhineland. On 12 June 1961, Scheliha, who had been appointed adviser to the Department of Justice, gave a speech to the Rotary Club in S. on 'Justice and Crime'.

Excerpts from the Discussion

(*Applause*)

THE PRESIDENT OF THE ROTARY CLUB: He would like to thank the Honorable Mr Scheliha for his remarks. Nevertheless, he would like to point out that there was a definite appreciation of justice and injustice among Rotarians. Furthermore, there were some things one should not think about too much. ROTARIAN BENGER-RIBANA: The Speaker had called the hussar's tunic an 'Attila'. The proper name for it is, of course, a 'Dolman'. The speech contained further examples of the speaker's inaccuracy. But a loosely formulated idea was not a correct idea when it concerned the unresolved past. ROT. PLETTKE: Legal problems always affected only a minority. ROT. BARABAS: As a penologist, he could not understand the speaker's pessimism. Speaking for himself, he was an optimist in such matters.

(*Applause*)

There was one important point which Mr Scheliha had not sufficiently considered: that of mercy. Wherever there was justice, there was also mercy; a justice not enriched with mercy was inconceivable, although in these days, of course, it was necessary to apply stricter standards when dealing with a person applying for a pardon.

(*Loud applause*)

Basic Discussion

ROT. GEIBEL: He could not imagine that in 1953 the German people had been 'without values', as the speaker had maintained. German self-control and German values, in the words of the national anthem, did not perish even in 1945. ROT. PILS: If there was blood-guilt, it could not attach to the German people, since the crime had been committed in the province of West Prussia. Hence it attached to Poland. ROT. WALLER: It was impossible for a society to dissolve, even with the consent of all its members, Kant's example was therefore utopian. ROT. HENN: If he might be permitted to speak from his experience in the Bundestag: it had been shown repeatedly that, particularly in cases of treason, serious philosophical factors must be taken into consideration. Experience had shown that lax punishment was the very thing which, in Kant's sense, wrought havoc upon a nation, or rather, wrought havoc from within the nation. ROT. GLAS: The German people had, after all, insisted on punishment at the time, it was only the apparatus which had failed to function. But Mr Scheliha himself had recommended moderation. He had cited the example merely on account of his change of attitude. ROT. VALENTIN: He failed to understand why no investigation had been made as to whether or not von Z. had acted in self-defence. ROT. MERTENS: As far as he knew, Infantry Regiment 71 had been in the environs of Klopau at the time. These troops could have been used to look for the murderer.

Intensified Discussion

PRESIDENT: Due to limitations of time, each member's remarks must be restricted to one minute. He therefore asked that comments be kept short. The discussion could continue. ROT. LAMBRECHT: What was meant by 'for each person to receive his just deserts'? Philosophically speaking, this must be regarded as a matter of practice. ROT. BISCHOF: Obviously it was a question of action. ROT. ERB: And as a doctor, one could not do other than support that view. ROT. KATRIN: All the same, there was no doubt whatever that it was better for one man to die than for a whole people to be dragged down. PRESIDENT: True; in principle, the Rotary Club was interested in social problems, but this was not, strictly speaking, a social problem. ROT. KATRIN: On the other hand, whether there was no longer any value in people speaking about the end, that was something he was doubtful about. ROT. JACOBY: One must concentrate on the problem itself. ROT. SCHMIDTHENNER: It was a matter of background and education. ROT. GLAUBE: If he might speak from experience: Frederick II, the King, that is to say, not the Emperor, had once said: The civil servant and the philosopher owed their strength to their detachment from reality. Today, however, he wished to speak not as a civil servant or a philosopher but as a practical man, and practice meant involvement in reality. Who was prepared these days, for example, to risk his life or his liberty for any particular problem of justice? ROT. SPRENGEL: The question of punishment raised by Kant was a very specific and perhaps misleading one. It was possible that a preventive measure on the part of the police was considerably more effective than any subsequent punishment. ROT. MAINZ: What was required was a state based not on legal procedure but on preventive justice, beginning with the police. Salazar had recognized this long ago. ROT. PATZAK: To come back to Kant: As a returning prisoner of war, it had been possible to observe that, even without punishment and 'values' in the Kantian sense, there had been development and progress. It was very difficult to recall the strange sense of impending disaster prevalent during the final months of the war (the only thing it might be compared to was the mood of deepening twilight in the pre-Christmas period).

On the Love of Justice

MR SCHELIHA: Punishment depended on the mood. In the same way, criminal investigation and crime itself were each dependent on the unity of time and space being maintained. Without a specific atmosphere, neither the crime nor the criminal investigation could succeed. PRESIDENT: He wished to thank the speaker for his address. ROT. PEICKERT: He had always considered justice to be one of the most nonsensical ideals. ROT. BALUNGA: He had always been interested in how justice could turn into crime and how crime could evade justice. These aspects should also be borne in mind when examining the problem. ROT. PILS: Justice was a totalitarian principle. ROT. WALLER: It was impossible however, to dispense with justice. The criminologist was the watchdog of legal security, the judge was king of the law. PRESIDENT: Would members kindly keep their remarks as brief as possible, as the time for fruitful discussion was limited. ROT. VON BERGMANN: An inordinate love of justice was reminiscent of perversion; in ancient times, there had even been defenders of homosexuality. ROT. EBER: It was strange that the term justice occurred frequently in texts from classical antiquity. ROT. FÜRBRINGER: We must have justice! Without it, life would be impossible. ROT. SCHUMPETER: How could he prove it, though? PRESIDENT: No interruptions, please: Mr Fürbringer has the floor.

Conclusion

ROT. LEBSIUS: The problem discussed today had been most stimulating. The problems involved in the administration of justice had been brought to light in a very productive manner. ROT. PICHOTA: The logical nature of the address had left a great impression. ROT. ARNDT: At last we have had some plain speaking.

(*Lively applause*)

PRESIDENT: Now that the discussion had yielded many stimulating ideas, he requested the speaker to make his concluding comments. MR SCHELIHA: He thanked the members for this opportunity of speaking to them. PRESIDENT: Time was running out, he would like to thank Mr Scheliha in the name of all those present for his appropriate and enlightening remarks.

(*Hearty and prolonged applause*)

FRÄULEIN VON POSA

I

The young mistress of the manor, Fräulein von Posa, had the gates to the road shut so no one would come into the yard. Later she changed her mind and had the gates opened again. She gave instructions to the kitchen to feed the people who poured into the yard. Smoke hung over the town, the upper layers had been broken off by the wind.

Dr von Posa was waiting in the drawing room for his coffee. Radio Luxembourg was broadcasting a reasonably good operatic concert. Fräulein von Posa tried to reach the Cathedral dean in town, but this was impossible, all telephone connections with the town having been cut because the enemy was so close. She felt guilty for having wanted to keep the gates to the yard closed. Throughout the day, airplanes passed overhead from west to east. As dive bombers approached the estate, Miss Posa ran behind the barns to the air-raid shelter reserved for members of the family. She hardly knew what she was doing as she ran. On the camp cot, which took up most of the room in the small bunker, lay the Pole and Gloria. Miss Posa sat down beside them on the edge of the cot and stopped them from getting up out of embarrassment. Instead, she gathered up their articles of clothing which lay strewn around. The young Pole sat between the two women. Gloria began, rather brazenly, to get dressed in front of her sister. Miss Posa busied herself all day with the people who had settled down in the yard and the barns and were being fed. Later, the chairman of the Rural District Council arrived with some of his men and resumed the search for the runaway Pole. They found him this time, he had become careless and was wandering behind the barns. The chairman of the Rural District Council had him handcuffed and interrogated him.

Towards evening, American tanks approached the town, whence the long-drawn-out sound of a siren was to be heard. Miss Posa was occupied with the labourers and foreign workers coming in from the fields in small groups. They were avid for news. By evening, the young foreign worker, Gloria's Pole, had disappeared. During the night, two women who were in labour were brought in from the town, and Miss Posa had to persuade her father to accept them: he could not afford to turn them down—but he had got into the habit of letting himself be persuaded. The births also kept Gloria busy, for she had to cut the umbilical cord, the only thing Dr von Posa could not bring himself to do. That was Liberation Day.

II

After it became certain that the Pole would not return, Miss Posa gradually relaxed. The night following the arrival of the Allies, she could not fall asleep, so she got dressed and began to tidy up the house. She collected the numerous crosses and statuettes of Jesus which made her uneasy, and put them all in one spot. She was afraid to see them in their accustomed places. She desired passionately to be good again. She saw incredulously that there were circumstances which made it impossible to be good yet offered no compensation. What was to happen? She suffered a crisis during the night and prayed (crouched in an armchair). Then she wept until she fell asleep.

Continence

She could have taken this young foreign worker for her lover—he had access to the manor because only in the manor could he be safely hidden. Why didn't she take him? Her continence drove the man into the arms of her little sister, whom she ought to have protected better.

Reaction to the Disappearance of the Young Foreign Worker

Miss Posa shed some of the malaise of the last few days when she was sure she would not find him again; nevertheless, she looked for him till it was dark. She drove to the various foreign workers' quarters, where freedom celebrations were gradually getting under way, and asked for him. He had not been seen anywhere.

Vampire Father

Ever since these glorious sunny spring days had set in, she had a vague, passionate desire which could have been channelled in any direction, but the only outlet for that goodwill was her father, who appropriated what he could get of it. He exploited her in his practice, where she sterilized instruments for him, or sent her on errands to neighbouring estates or into town, to shop for specialties at the delicatessen stores.

Dr von Posa

Ernst, born 1886, studied medicine, became a doctor like his father before him. Everyone prophesied a brilliant career for Ernst von Posa. In 1914, became deputy superintendent of Field Hospital No. 3 in Lemberg, a clearing station for the wounded of the rapidly retreating 3rd army of General of the Cavalry, von Brudermann. Posa was caught in the Przemysl trap, where he had managed to salvage portions of his Lemberg hospital. Within a few days, the encircled stronghold of Przemysl was doomed. As a Russian prisoner of war, Posa was exchanged via Denmark for captured Russian doctors. In 1916, he visited the battlefield of 16 September 1914, at the Oise, where two of Posa's brothers were buried. Had the Zouaves cut out their eyes?

The war over, his only desire was for the 'finer things of life'. Visited Mallorca and Ibiza in 1921; Tunis and Greece in 1923; travelled through Portugal and Spain in 1928; married Brigitte von D. in 1920, divorced six years later. Various Mediterranean voyages in 1932, 1935, 1936, 1937, 1939 (in the spring), including Corfu. Country practice and maternity home at the Posa estate. Extremely sensitive to cold. Since Przemysl unable to tolerate hunger, hence his daily schedule punctuated by numerous small meals. Short-tempered with patients. Plays the violin.

Turning Point

As far back as February, Fräulein von Posa had been hoping for a turning point in her personal relations and intentions. She noticed that something inside her was getting ready. She was familiar with these presentiments from previous occasions, and calculated that, after the nadir of the last few years, there was bound to be an upward trend.

Corpse-Recovery Detail

For a long time, Miss Posa found no opportunity of doing anything except: feeding people who would otherwise have got their food elsewhere, until she received an offer to take charge of a corpse-recovery detail. She accepted this assignment, and with the aid of her men (farm labourers, workers supplied by the civic authorities) searched the ruined town for corpses. On the third day, fortified with brandy to enable them endure the stench, they found a cellar under the rubble. It contained 60 bodies. In addition, they found isolated corpses, bodies charred to the size of an arm, also some that had merely been buried under the rubble and so looked normal, all of which they transported to mass graves supplied by the civic authorities. Fräulein von Posa asked for one week's leave for her men during which she wanted to clear a bombed church with them. This was refused at the insistence of the health authorities. During this time, Miss Posa often thought of the young Pole.

Search for Something Good

After the recovery detail had also cleared up the civic theatre site, it was disbanded and not put to work rebuilding churches, as Fräulein von Posa had requested. So she roamed the streets searching for something good to do. But her efforts with the military-occupation authorities merely led to misunderstandings, which she was unable to clarify because she lacked the necessary experience. There was no market for what she had in mind. For a month, she observed signs of pregnancy on her body. But a pregnancy was impossible. Gloria confessed to her that she had committed an indiscretion with the Pole. She talked to Gloria about the Pole and kissed her sister when they talked about him. After their conversation, she felt an even stronger desire for something good.

III

The Posa family migrated from the Netherlands to Jülich-Cleve in the seventeenth century. Living in this province, the family became part of Prussia. During the first siege of Mainz, a Lieutenant von Posa, under the eyes of his Elector, prevented the slaughter of a civilian in the village of Bretzenheim. In 1793, a member of the

Pomeranian branch of the von Posa family went over to the French revolutionary troops and was executed by a firing squad after the occupation of Paris in 1815. In 1848, J. H. von Kirchheim, vice president of the Superior Assize Court in Ratibor from 1836 to 1851 (his mother was a von Posa), cancelled the warrant for the arrest of Count Reichenbach. The King of Prussia wrote to him: Do not understand ruling, herewith express my dissatisfaction. Von Kirchheim was given five years' leave of absence. As a deputy in the Prussian Diet, von Kirchheim raised constitutional objections to measures of this kind. On his way back, he was forcibly retired on grounds of discreditable behaviour. The four Posas then in Prussian service as magistrates and army officers resigned their posts. Later generations of the Posa family provided doctors only. In 1871, it was Surgeon-General Franz von Posa who drew the attention of Lieutenant-General von Voigt-Rhetz to the butcher Steinmetz during the battle of St Privat. The following day, Steinmetz was replaced by another military commander.

Eight von Posas and von Kirchheims took part in the First World War. The eccentric advance of the Austro-Hungarian armies to the north beyond Lemberg cost most of them their lives. They fell as Prussian liaison and medical officers in the armies of Brudermann and Dankl and as members of the Prussian auxiliary force Woersch. Two other von Posas fell shortly afterward in the west, after accomplishing nothing. The only one to survive the First World War was the shell-shocked Ernst von Posa on the Posa estate in northern Hesse. During the next few years, the Posa family suffered a crisis. The surviving and younger generations of Posas: the same mouth, shadows around the mouth, the same inquisitive eyes, dark golden-brown, prematurely greying hair, temples throbbing when excited, veins at the temples—just like the Posas around 1700, around 1800, around 1900, but now in a crisis.

IV

What Is Good (bonum)?

Not the Fatherland, Europe—which Europe? The soothing of pain, misfortune, brings no relief. To abstain from wrongdoing—what does that mean? A Posa commits no wrongs. The truth? Tell it to whom? Continence—no. What, then, is good? The family estates? Yes. But that cannot be all.

Lieutenant von Hacke (a Posa on His Mother's Side)

Love for the inherited estates near Brunswick was the undoing of Ernst von Hacke. Returning as a major from the First World War (last in Hamburg, 1919, liquidation of artillery horse stocks at a considerable profit for the Treasury), he hoped to acquire the funds necessary for the maintenance of the estates by working without pay in the banking firm of Traeger, Peickert & Co. (relations of his wife). Tips from banking friends in Munich prompted him to enter into speculations in which he lost additional moneys. The encumbered estates were placed under trusteeship. From 1928 to 1930, Major von Hacke studied singing in Hanover. His first instructor, court singer Merkel von Karonin, had expressed himself optimistically about his career in this field. Von Hacke threw himself into this new life, which seemed to offer rich spoils. In the following years, the name Hacke appeared in the musical programmes of Coburg, Halberstadt, Kottbus, Torgau, Brandenburg and Danzig, but never prominently. Von Hacke avoided the Brunswick area. In 1935, Hacke was recalled to the Wehrmacht. On 1 September 1935, he took up his duties at the war ministry in Berlin with the rank of lieutenant colonel. Posted in remote headquarters, he missed the Polish and Western campaigns. He saw his chance of saving the estates if he distinguished himself in this war.

In 1941, friends obtained for him one of the then most effective implements of the army: the 2nd Lower Saxon Panzer regiment. This fine regiment went with the 44th armoured unit to northern Russia. Fair Saxon craniums looked out of well-equipped tank turrets. Special apparatus of all kinds was at his disposal. As commanding officer of this weapon, von Hacke could, theoretically speaking, count on being decorated: even the Knight's Cross with Oak Leaves seemed within reach. The decorations would have freed him from all anxiety, for it was improbable that such a distinguished soldier would later be left at the mercy of his debts. However, before a single engagement with the enemy, the regiment's vehicles entered a wide expanse of swampland. The regiment had to be escorted back in the midst of the offensive. One week later, the regiment, now being utilized on a different front sector, saw itself abandoned by the accompanying infantry regiments. En route to Leningrad, its flanks were attacked right and left. The Panzers had no choice but to retreat. Von Hacke stood weeping with his officers beside the plank road, watching the tanks, mounted with grenadiers, rumbling back; meanwhile, from the sides, desperate defence action on the part of the machine-gun units, who were trying to give the regiment a chance.

Winter and spring were likewise devoid of success. Hacke's Panzer regiment, hitherto operating independently, was reincorporated into a new division. For a time, von Hacke fought in vain in the Crimea. Because of these failures, Hacke-Posa did not take part in the officers' conspiracies of 1943/44. In Croatia, he was given a gendar-merie regiment which, however, had to grapple with insurmountable problems. Even extraordinary success could no longer have led to promotion or decorations in this remote theatre of war. A liaison during the furlough in the Reich capital caused new debts to accumulate there. At that point, an English air raid mistakenly destroyed the object of all these efforts: the Herford estate. Hacke, now promoted to colonel, knew nothing of this when the request of one of his friends reached him to take part in the relief of Budapest. So he advanced with his unit on Budapest. His attacks from the south-west confused the attackers and the attacked; it was expected that the city would be relieved from Lake Balaton. After two days, the regiment, mentioned specifically in the dispatches of the Supreme Command, withdrew once more to the Yugoslavian border.

For a variety of reasons, this stroke of luck came too late. (The indebtedness of the von Hacke estates did not improve until the currency reform.) Von Hacke took over command of a divisional headquarters in the Chositz valley. The division expected from Greece, of which this headquarters was supposed to assume command, never materialized. The staffs of Hacke, Fehn and Kobe, all of whom were in the valleys of former Herzegovina, trying to decide whether to break through to the American lines or surrender to the partisans, negotiated with partisan leaders in Krtic-Chositz. During the night, the partisan leaders fled, believing themselves to be in danger. A heavily armed tank column, carrying the staffs of Fehn, Kobe and Hacke, reached the American lines near Klagenfurt but were turned back. This was no laughing matter. A few days later, von Hacke, Fehn and Kobe were executed.

Baroness von Posa

During the night of 2 to 3 January 1945, Baroness von Posa was relieved of her conscience. The conscience: an ordinary cash box containing the von Posa family jewels. Erika von Posa had sent the cash box by registered mail from the Posa estate in eastern Germany to Nuremberg, as soon as friends in Supreme Command had informed her that the Russians were approaching Posa. The cash box arrived safely in Nuremberg and, as agreed at the outbreak of the war, was being held by a pharmacist's family at the 'Golden Star' (as the venerable pharmacy was called). The Baroness herself held out too long on the estate. She and her farm wagons got caught up among retreating German troops. In the 1920s, she had driven to Berlin with these wagons and farm hands from the old Posa estate near Stolpe and supervised functions of the German People's Party in Berlin. Now, during the first days of snow, she lost her farm hands, the foreign workers and the wagons. Her own wagon was pushed off the side of the road by armoured vehicles. After she was flung out, a wagon wheel rolled across her shins. Soldiers carried her on a stretcher to a field hospital. She turned up in Nuremberg as a cripple who could only get about in a wheelchair, that is, unless she wanted to crawl. During the night of 2 to 3 January 1945, the city of Nuremberg was attacked by Allied bombers. The 'Golden Star' was hit by incendiaries and high-explosive bombs. Baroness von Posa and the owners of the building spent the hours of the attack in the lower vaults of the 'Star'. Five fully finished basement levels contained medical supplies, alcohol and dressings. When the occupants of the cellar noticed smoke seeping in, they broke through the bricked-up entrance that led to the catacombs of the old section of Nuremberg. With her conscience pressed against her ageing body, Erika von Posa tried to crawl to the gap in the wall through which the owners had escaped. The bricked-up entrance was separated from the cellar level by an 18-inch threshold. The baroness fell from that sill into the catacomb passage, which was considerably lower. Her poorly mended shinbones broke. Some looters turned up out of the darkness after she had been shouting for help for some hours and took away her sole possession, the cash box with her conscience.

The baroness spent the years 1945 to 1948 in the Gartenstadt refugee camp in northern Bavaria, where the Nuremberg air-raid victims had first been taken. Her nephew, André von Teck, returned from a Russian prisoner-of-war camp in 1949. He took the baroness to live with him in his home in Wiesbaden. The cash box turned up later at a jeweller's; the baroness denied it was hers. Her leg bones grew together again. Baroness von Posa declined to move about to any appreciable extent.

Police Commissioner von Kirchheim

Von Kirchheim's way of looking at things (he was born in 1906) was that of logic. The logical way of looking at things corresponds to that of internal administration. It regards the state as a machine: however, this leads not to a simplified view but to inventiveness, if this machinery of administration and police is to be adapted to individual requirements and realities. In 1923, von Kirchheim entered the service of the Prussian Internal Administration. In 1929, he switched to the police branch. 1933 found him in Breslau investigating a murder. On 28 January, Kirchheim ordered the arrest of the perpetrators, who were Brownshirts. Within a few days, Group Leader Heines was made Chief of Police in Breslau and Governor of Silesia. On 6 February, trade union leaders were shot in their apartments. After the March elections, Commercial Counselor Jägerlein, together with a member of the local district council, was found shot. Two labour leaders were found dead on 16 March. Brownshirts appeared in the apartment of Secretary Lindau and started shooting. When the journalist König left a house in the Breitenstrasse one evening, his face was slashed with a razor. In these cases, von Kirchheim appeared at the scene of the crime accompanied by reliable police officials. To the wife of a trade union leader who requested protection for various union members, he replied: What do you expect us to do? We can hardly protect ourselves.

What is the meaning of bravery at a time when all that matters is not to be trampled to death? Von Kirchheim did not find the right moment for the traditional brave deed. In 1941, von Kirchheim was appointed inspector for the border area between Lithuania and East Prussia. There were cases of overlapping authority to be cleared up. Von Kirchheim produced a report containing important suggestions for manpower and material savings in these areas; moreover, the report was of basic significance for other border areas where overlapping occurred. Later in Allenstein he heard that incidents had taken place in the border area during his tour of inspection about which he had not been told. In the 'weeding-out process', there were 201 dead in Garsden, 288 in Krottingen, 191 in Polangen, 255 in Taurroggen, 322 in Georgenburg, 192 in Wladislawa, 68 in Mariampol, 230 in Wirballen, 150 in Calvaria, 300 in Wilkowischen, and an undetermined number in Szewekzwie and Vebirzewiai. Those were murders. Von Kirchheim went to Berlin and lodged complaints with the Ministry of the Interior. For the time being, he was given no further assignment. Later, he was given a police regiment in the Caucasus for whose achievements he was awarded the Knight's Cross. His deplorable behaviour at the Ministry of the Interior appeared to have been forgotten. But then, in the autumn of 1944, von K. was executed. It later turned out that the occasion for adopting the attitude which cost him his life had been ill chosen, for the excesses in the border areas had already been stopped from another source. But which moment, which situation, from among the onslaught of events since 1933 would have been a more appropriate one for Kirchheim's intervention?

The Ambitious Gerda von Posa-Esebeck

Cousin Gerda was found guilty by a criminal court in Kattowitz of impersonating a Red Cross nurse (she was underage and not permitted to wear a Red Cross uniform). She had been recognized from the description in Nos 1044–1046 of the German Police Gazette, according to which she was of slight build, 16 years old but carrying papers proclaiming her to be 22. She wore an Iron Cross Class II to which she was not entitled. The officials identified her from the description. A spurious Red Cross nurse had turned up in Rottenburg, Munich, Gleiwitz, Guben, Leipzig, Jena, Hanover, Kreiensen, Halberstadt, Goslar, Strasbourg, Essen, Freiburg, Schneidemühl, Danzig, Allenstein and Litzmannstadt. It was for this Red Cross nurse that Gerda von Posa was mistaken. She was convicted of a number of misdemeanours and sentenced to two years in prison.

The Unfortunate First Lieutenant von Posa

His promotion to the rank of first lieutenant nearly came to nought as a result of his argumentative streak. In the presence of Field Marshal von Reichenau, he criticized the Army's training methods. The Field Marshal laughed. Since the officers who were present interpreted it as a benevolent laugh, the first lieutenant was not demoted to the rank of second lieutenant. A few weeks later, young Posa found himself taking part in the skirmish at Feodosia on the Black Sea. The term battle is permissible where the number of dead on both sides amounts to 1,200; at Feodosia, 16 soldiers fell on the Russian side and 240 on the German. A heavy Russian cruiser appeared in Feodosia harbour during the night of 26 to 27 December 1941. They trained their naval searchlights on the German gun emplacements. Later, 23,000 men landed, touching off the well-known crisis on the Kerch Peninsula which cost Corps Commander von Sponeck his life and the 46th Infantry Division its honour. It was in these unfortunate circumstances that von Posa, who came through the fighting alive, found himself involved. No further reformist ideas were accepted from him. In 1943, he went over to the Russians.

Fräulein von Posa

Born 28 March 1922, on the Posa estate, the daughter of Dr E. von Posa: Nata von Posa. Charged with the care of her younger sister, Gloria von Posa. Searching for some good she can do; as the spring of 1945 approaches, turning-point imminent, great expectations combine with the new year. Frequent attendance at church, though the church building is burnt out and only a temporary shed is available. If she had been asked unexpectedly what she really meant by 'being good', she would not have known how to answer. She was a small part of the confused Posa family. But she was sure she would think of an answer. It had to be soon. It had to be this spring. She prayed fervently.

V

In the autumn of 1945, N. von Posa became the business representative of the Care Parcel organization for the district of Hesse. This had some remote connection with being good, at least it was a charitable enterprise. She was paid a suitable annual salary. In exchange, she sacrificed the much-hoped-for turning-point. Sacrifices of this kind were familiar to her: what it amounted to was that she capitulated once more, as she had done at various times in the past: it would have been foolish not to take advantage of the opportunity.

E. SCHINCKE

(a Patriot of Classical Ancient Latin)

I

In the years immediately following 1933, Eberhard Schincke, 48 years old, allowed himself to be duped by Hitler. He had read *The Threat to German Ideals* but believed that the National Socialist movement contained a core of idealism which the author of the book had failed to perceive. Schincke was prejudiced against the aristocracy of the intellect. He was the principal of the cathedral school in the small town of S. The younger members of his staff, Reh, Mortchen and Neumann, stood politically to the right of the National Socialists. The other teachers voted for the State Party. Schincke felt instinctively attracted by the National Socialists, more so than by the positions his colleagues took. He thought, as Nietzsche has taught us to do, not only with his head but also with all his senses, just as one uses more than one sense to grasp the meaning of a word, or as a woman becomes something more than an abstract quantity to the one who embraces her. Needless to say, Schincke's highly developed powers of perception were particularly bothered by the marching columns in the streets, but these were the expression, not the essence, of the movement. On the other hand, with his corpulent, elephantine build, his slouching, stoop-shouldered way of sitting, he was bound to make an unfavourable impression on the Brownshirts, although as it happened this deviation from the norm was part of the Germanic heritage, for, according to one of the most ancient Germanic sayings, the truly strong man is lethargic.

A dangerous situation developed one evening when some Brownshirts lay in wait for him; but apparently this was due to a misunderstanding which was cleared up the following day. Schincke had vague expectations of this movement, the birth of a new Romanticism which, instead of being confined to a small cultural élite, would share its wealth with the masses. He realized that these masses were perhaps not suited to develop quality on their own, but an outdoor performance of *Die Meistersinger* towards the end of 1933 in front of the cathedral, attended by a large number of the inhabitants who roasted sausages in the intermission, reconciled him and made him tingle with optimism, as opera was now climbing down into the world, so to speak, and real life was acquiring the same significance as life on the stage. It was in this state of mind that he got married in 1934. He saw, of course, that the provinces remained provincial, although on a bigger scale. He was hopeful, and at the same time concerned that the early upheaval might actually consolidate the narrowness of life there, but it was not his way to complain about something which did not cause him any immediate inconvenience. It would have required a very powerful incentive to get him and his heavy body to oppose his entire environment, which provided him after all with his livelihood—and which the Third Reich embraced with the totality of a Hegelian concept. As with the great democracies of modern times, or some of the great scholars of the nineteenth century, it was as difficult to arouse his wrath as his willingness to condemn. His colleague Neumann could become indignant at a moment's notice. The university professors who became indignant about the National Socialists were more unpleasant than the National Socialists themselves. Schincke was moving along a quiet river on great floating islands of knowledge and emotion, for the most part kindly disposed towards the passing landscape. In 1934, he did not feel in the least like opposing something that did not directly threaten him, as long as it was only a nuisance. He was the close friend of a number of National Socialists whom he regarded as the paragons who would determine the future. The new education policy pursued by the Minister of Cultural Affairs, himself a philologist, worked to the advantage of both Schincke and the school. The classical section of the region's historical society, of which Schincke was chairman, now received considerable financial grants. It was finally possible to stop dabbling and get down to serious study.

For some years, Schincke had been researching the cultural reforms of Charlemagne. It was more than mere disorientation that motivated his interest in this remote material. He felt there was clear evidence that the quadruple constellation of Charlemagne, Alcuin, Theodulf and Arn had produced a cultural nucleus of which, within 30 short years, nothing but fossils remained. It was the brief life of this precious plant to which he wanted to give literary form and whose laws of existence he wanted to describe. The story of the decline of a culture within 30 years was a subject fit for a classical history of ethics. But there was also the fascination of a culture being created out of nothing—for what prior culture could have existed among the barbaric Franks? This was to be the subject of a paper. Granted, he could also have taken contemporary material to develop his ideas, but he did not feel qualified to do so. Moreover, he would have been afraid his ideas might interfere with a still-living culture. That was why he preferred to develop his ideas around an example of which there was nothing left to destroy. Another factor was his aversion to topicality, acquired after many years of study, a taboo which he did not regard as binding but to which he nevertheless adhered.

Schincke was now given an assistant for his research; the school acquired a gymnasium which could also double up as a concert hall. The assistant was later recalled, however. The favourable attitude adopted by the government towards classical philology and medieval research proved to be an integral part of the familiar programme of pacification: it is best for the mind to occupy itself with ancient or medieval history, that being less dangerous than a preoccupation with the present. Since the end of 1935 and the beginning of 1936, Schincke could be duped no more by the movement and no longer yielded to its blandishments. But what was he to do? By way of contrast with his usual lethargy it could be said that, once roused, he became a menace. But what was the good of being a menace if he was unarmed? After all, he could not cane the object of his wrath, and what he wrote in his diary nobody read. During the 1936 Easter holidays, he participated in his last obligatory manoeuvres as a captain in the Reserve. He spent his time feeling cold and fighting off stomach upsets. During the final parade of the regiments taking part in manoeuvres outside the town of Qu., he stood to one side of General von Witzleben. One after another, the officers riding at the head of the advancing columns of regiments left their positions, galloped in a semicircle up to the Commander-in-Chief and saluted. Colonel F. had difficulty in getting his horse, which had adjusted its pace to the other officers' horses, to gallop; at the salute, the General coldly dismissed him. While all this was going on, Schincke was shivering on the great parade ground where the wind blew unimpeded; like all the others, he was mounted on a large horse, and not properly equipped for the ordeal. He did not think he would ever forget that terrible day. He observed these manoeuvres, and he ceased to believe in the victory of the National Socialists.

During the remainder of April and May, Schincke had to make were trips and instructional visits as a representative of the Department of Education; in June, he was occupied with reorganizing seminar courses for new teachers. In July, complicated libel proceedings between numerous members of the teaching staff had to be headed off; an internal crisis among the faculty overburdened by the demands of adjusting to the new era. His research took up all his time during August. In September, he was given a lectureship at the nearby university; in addition, he was put in charge of reorganizing the recently established training centre for new teachers. What else could he have done? He was not trained to have a *fait accompli* such as the Third Reich for an enemy.

As the year went on and one activity gave way to the next—had it been a question of pupils, one might have called it occupational therapy—Schincke's thoughts continued to flow quietly along. Under the surface, however, the accumulation of minor irritations and observations led to a sudden eruption of antipathy towards the movement which he had hitherto trusted. Many National Socialist colleagues and university professors now found themselves out of favour. He still hoped the fresh tide of 1933 might return on a modified level, if, for example, Hitler ceased to be distracted by foreign policy; meanwhile, he became increasingly hostile to the representatives of this new order. He read fragments from Thomas Mann's *Lotte in Weimar*, brought in from Switzerland, and collected rational explanations for the failure of the National Socialist revolution which was developing into a state of athletes and patriots. He read a great deal of Nietzsche. This all took place, of course, only in his mind. No one knew anything about his change of attitude. He was not talkative. He did discuss it with his young wife, because he could trust her. Schincke had been brought up to take the separation between idea and reality for granted. He could get along with mental reservations for a long time. An intellectual lives in the past and future just as much as the present, and for him the present is also what is impossible at present, that which has, so to speak, been destroyed by the present; in other words, he can also live in an unborn present, but this requires a strict separation between private and public life. However, the system of channelling essence and reality, his old recipe, did not work with the constant interplay of all spheres of life under this system. Schincke approved, generally speaking, of this aspect of the new system, since he naturally considered it right and proper for lying to be made difficult and truth to be made easy; nevertheless, his allergy to the details of this practice continued to grow. The annual rhythm of conferences and assignments—he enjoyed the reputation of a philological luminary—gave him less and less pleasure. Nor could he get around the problem of large numbers. In earlier years, he had dealt with the small circle of his school; now he was occupied with hundreds of National Socialists and non-National Socialists, whom he could not love because he virtually did not know them. His wife could not understand why he maintained the separation between his actual functions and his feelings. She believed—just as on principle she believed in the unity of the personality—in gradually adjusting feelings to activities, which after all had been their original state. She thought he should make a greater effort with his feelings. As she saw it: reality could not be changed, so she argued in favour of adjusting one's ideas. But Schincke's ideas were firmly anchored, secured by many references and determined by a precise and definite taste on which he claimed to have no influence. The discord between the inner and the outer man, which could be neither maintained nor resolved, caused him physical pain. He would have liked to become ill. He was overburdened. But he did not become ill, he became careless instead. Like the old gentlemen whose verbose opposition to the system he ridiculed, he became garrulous.

In the winter of 1941, Schincke was relieved of his post on account of political utterances concerning the outcome of the war. He was saved from prison by National Socialist friends outside S., whose influence was just about sufficient for this. His colleagues Neumann, Reh and Wirth cut him publicly once the dismissal was announced. Neumann became his successor. The classical section of the historical society did not re-elect him. During this time, his wife's and his closest friend G., a stage designer at the municipal theatre, was forcibly drafted, i.e. the police took him from his apartment after his unsuccessful attempt to run away. G., who had abnormal inclinations, could not possibly endure the constant proximity of rough, normal, sometimes foul-smelling men. A few weeks after he was drafted, he suffered a nervous breakdown. He was taken to a military hospital in Dresden. The doctors thought he was bluffing, and when G. tried to escape from the hospital, he was court martialled for desertion and shot. His wife, Frau Schincke's bosom friend, after making several last-minute journeys to try and save her husband, took poison when she was told. These weeks, in which he failed to save his friend, led to a temporary separation between Schincke and his wife, who could not believe that her husband was completely powerless, or rather—her actions were seldom dictated by only one motive—could not love a man who, accustomed as he was to an enormous expenditure of mental energy every day for many years, could accomplish nothing in an emergency such as this. She went to Karlsbad Spa but returned six months later, pregnant by an officer of the intelligence corps. Husband and wife agreed on an abortion, and after the operation lived together in their suburban villa. All Schincke had to live on was his pension and their ration cards. He found it hard to reduce his standards because he had never been really poor. He could not lead the cramped existence of a retired teacher. He would have gladly gone to the front now, but his application was rejected, on grounds of poor physical condition, by a first lieutenant who disliked him and who, like the town's entire upper crust, cut him. Schincke had no connections in the industrial world. The local party headquarters kept him busy with menial jobs, such as distributing food coupons and checking supplies. There he sat, every month, exposed to public humiliation, doling out food coupons. He tried to get his doctor to declare him medically unfit, but the doctor refused to give him any certificate at all. From time to time he suffered hunger pangs, his large body required large quantities of food. He was overtaxed. His duties as an air-raid warden, of which, having no occupation, he was allotted more than most people, prevented him from getting enough sleep. He was in a state in which he was liable to burst into tears if someone spoke to him suddenly. He had long since given up hope that this misery would ever end. He thought of nothing but sabotage, and he made up his mind that, at the next provocation, he would refuse to work and face the consequences. The contempt he was shown from all sides debilitated him and rendered him incapable of continuing his private research. He had lost faith in it. The 20th of July and the subsequent executions frightened him. He would not have believed they would dare kill traitors occupying such exalted positions. He thought the persecution might also affect him, although since 1941 he had been consistently careful, and was afraid of being mistaken for a member of the Resistance. He was incapable of getting down to any work at all. His wife found it impossible to remain with him and went back to Karlsbad.

The inactivity and the feeling of being treated more and more like an old man had made him so despondent that he regarded the air raid which finally hit S. in March 1945 as a welcome breach of the anathema under which he had been placed. Bombs also fell in the vicinity of Schincke's villa. Schincke emerged from his cellar even before the air raid was over; he was in time to see a group of airplanes flying off. After a brief inspection of his house, which was undamaged, he ran along the dishevelled avenue of chestnuts towards the town. On the outskirts, party members were piloting the inhabitants fleeing town. The garrison had left the barracks and were occupying the smoke-filled intersections, which were strewn with broken concrete and splinters and from which one could see a short distance into the burning rows of houses, in the sidestreets. There were onlookers, as if there had been a traffic accident. People carrying homemade preserves hurried through the smoke towards the intersections, in danger from burning housefronts that could collapse at any moment. From one corner to the next, Schincke pushed his way towards his old school. He was hoping the school's great cool cellars, which he could not imagine would ever be destroyed, might offer some protection from the almost unbearable heat. The school had been hit by bombs, but was only partially destroyed. The pupils, taken unawares by the air raid while they were in class, were waiting in the yard for instructions from the principal's office. The principal could not decide what to do. Neumann concealed this lack of decision by activity. The telephone service was disrupted and instructions from the school board were unobtainable. After a time, messengers arrived from city hall with an evacuation order for the whole school, as the children could not remain in the town. From the Lower Town, consisting of medieval timbered buildings, a wide wall of fire was approaching Cathedral Square. Men were retreating across the square towards the school, where they tried to set up headquarters. Trucks driven by soldiers appeared in the school yard, with orders to remove the pupils. Two hundred people were said to be buried in the air-raid shelter at St Paul's. Principal Neumann gave instructions to the soldiers who reported to him and divided the boys into groups for transportation.

Schincke, who had turned up at first as a mere spectator and out of affection for his old school, was delighted to find himself included in the transportation arrangements. After his wretched years of banishment, this seemed to him somehow like a historic moment of national unity, an evocation of the spirit of 1806; he had forgotten that he wanted to do nothing further for these people. Neumann gave him instructions, assigned a private and a driver to him and with their help was to transport two classes by truck to a specified rendezvous. Thanks to his familiarity with the area, he managed to guide the convoy out of the ruined town along a sandy track beside the river.

As night fell, however, Schincke lost his way. His convoy failed to arrive at the agreed rendezvous, where the school was to assemble and receive further instructions. He gave orders to halt at a spot which was unfamiliar even to him, right next to a barn, no village in sight; a few hundred yards away, a highway, unmarked, led past this barn; a path connected the two. The next morning, after spending the night with his pupils in the barn, Schincke felt no urge whatever to get back on the proper route. Not for anything did he want to resume the life of the years 1941 to 1944. He was not prepared to lift a finger for the appalling life he had led during the last few years.

II

My friend Carlton has just returned. I heard the truck coming along the path to the barn. He is talking outside to the boys. I shan't go out. What would I say? I could only say I am glad to see them making friends, and I would feel like my wife when she tries to couple people she is in love with.

I confided in Carlton yesterday. It intoxicates me when he puts his head down to me, his ear close to me.

A reserve officer is supposed to be able to read maps, but I have always been more of a pedagogue, and, if it had been possible to be that without also being a reserve officer, I would have cheerfully foregone the annual training periods. In any event, I have never been much good at map-reading; a fact that has now brought us to quite a different destination from the one planned. If it didn't sound so absurd, I would say that, with the mistake we made, we have divorced ourselves from events.

Carlton agreed at once. He put a few questions, on which I seized avidly, but these questions were soon settled: I had been expecting questions which would have confirmed the reality of my plan to me. But I grabbed at the questions too hastily (soup bowl upset in eagerness). Carlton let himself be deceived by my plan, for it was only his attentive listening that made it sound so convincing. He said he thought no one could be so convinced of anything unless it were necessary, and that anyone who has so much to say in favour of a plan must himself be convinced of it.

I have never been through anything like it. But I would not want to sacrifice any of the terrible things that happened during the past few days. The air raid (pressed crouching against the cellar steps)—but when I ran through the torn-up town towards my old school, what was uppermost in my mind was that I would be able to tell my wife all about it. My realization: a disaster becomes truly terrible only when you no longer feel enriched by the experience. Hence also the old boredom as soon as I am out of danger, the familiar fatigue when I am in the country. It's not the country that is to blame, it's the change of environment forcing me to leave behind familiar habits. Vague plans, painful, mutilated ideas, inactivity, till there is a new accumulation of habits to bury the daily round in; I would not have thought that the appalling dangers of the last few days would be followed by nothing but the malaise of the city-dweller in rural surroundings.

My heavy body is not suited to days like this. Too much surface that feels cold at night, missing my wife, etc. You have to shake yourself, as you shake a watch or bang a radio (bite your hand) to formulate an idea. A cup of strong coffee would do it, or a refreshing bath. But I can't go and stand under the pump. The icy water would mean a chill. I ought to have started doing it earlier, as N. did, he chops up the ice in the winter and steps down into the freezing hole.

But there's no sense in that either; since the effort to harden himself to the cold takes all my colleague's strength, it doesn't matter whether he hardens himself or not.

Now I have come outside after all to see why Carlton is talking so much. I did not hide my annoyance, for Carlton has been talking away at these boys; in my opinion, he is just inciting them and making them feel restless. I was disappointed, disappointed that he would rather spend his time with the boys, who have nothing of interest to tell him, than talk to me, who could be instructive about so many things! I felt betrayed and forsaken. It is the same feeling of destructive rage that makes me throw down my glass at a party and leave the room because I can't see my wife but can hear her laughing. I can hear her saying: 'What on earth's the matter? Come on, tell me what's wrong! How funny you are,' etc. . . .

Presently, Carlton came and sat down beside me, making me feel much better. I stayed where I was, leaning over my frail little table—five narrow boards slapped together—and went on working. If I leaned on it, it would collapse. Its frailty is reminiscent of Desdemona, and I don't suppose anyone has ever said that of a table before.

The Flight

Neumann pointed to where the trucks were and kept on talking to me about the route I was to take and the rendezvous with the rest of the school, but after the unexpected greeting, and in my fear that our conversation would suddenly be broken off, I was incapable of taking anything in. Some firefighters stood behind Neumann waiting for orders. He saw them and started to go across to them. He dismissed me with a 'my dear Schincke', he oozed charm. He was not really friendly. The strong expression which he gave to his face had been assumed in such a hurry that it didn't fit properly and overflowed its purpose when he said goodbye to me with a warm-hearted grimace as if we were a couple of pansies. But since this was meaningless, the smile was stuck there, completely out of place, like my sister's hat when it slipped sideways at our mother's funeral. The boys had mounted the trucks, and the older ones, who still remembered me, called out: 'Churchill! Churchill!' because since my expulsion, which of course the boys knew all about and which was discussed by their parents, they have no inhibitions about calling me by the name given me at some time or other by the boys. I threaded my way among the various vehicles. They were army trucks, I had two soldiers as my aides: a driver, with colourless hair, and Carlton, who is a private, first class, and who, when I first saw him, I thought I had seen somewhere before, although it turned out I was mistaken. I asked him: 'Everything OK?' I thought the children looked tired and overstimulated, probably too excited to sleep. They had each been given two blankets. I chatted with them for a bit, and after those hours of terror they were greedy for words and hung over the sides of the truck. I sat down between the driver and the private up front. The memory of how I had lost my head when the first bombs dropped was like a red warning light in front of me. It paralyses me when someone obeys me. Since I grew up with my mother, who can't give orders, I am used to listening and doing what is expected of me. I get all confused when I find myself in the role of someone who is supposed to give orders. I suspected the driver would take a wrong route out of laziness. I had the impression that he wanted to be independent of the map, in the hope of finding a shorter route. I hadn't quite caught what he and Carlton had been saying to each other, but I gathered they didn't agree—possibly about the direction. So I intervened when the driver seemed about to turn off and ordered him to drive straight on. The road seemed familiar, and since the two soldiers said nothing, I took it as a confirmation of my suspicion. Later I realized we had lost our way. That was my fault. I considered taking Carlton into my confidence. But here in the cab the engine was making such a racket that he couldn't understand a word I was saying and told the driver to stop, with the result that I lost my head and asked him for God's sake to drive on.

Hungry, no midday nap: I was cold, and numb from so much happening without a word being uttered. My nerves were making an appalling racket, indistinguishable from the unbearable noise of the engine. My new supply of enthusiasm and sympathy (which we use to warm up things before we take them into our heads) was now all used up. I tried to recall something warming, but my memories had become mired. I looked dully at the hairy arms of my companions—the fur of animals. We couldn't go on driving like this for ever. So I said: 'It's possible our destination may be changed. I'll let you know.'

'Don't you know where we're going?'

'Yes, I do, but I have to see first,' I replied.

It turned out later that the barn was our destination. I was not sure whether the driver was following my instructions. Both men were looking out for temporary quarters near the road. In my present situation I did not wish to be precise, so I deliberately expressed myself in vague terms, the way you begin to rectify a mistaken idea which you suspect is mistaken by defining it vaguely. The driver with the colourless hair and the insipid pale eyes reminded me of a violinist from my student days. I had chosen a seat in the front row at a concert, where no one normally sat, so as to be nearer the music. This man, from the back row of violinists: 'Why don't you sit even closer?' He went on repeating this till I moved to a row further back. I was worried that, if I fell asleep, my head would droop towards the driver's side and, if it rested on his shoulder, might give a quite inappropriate impression of familiarity. Thinking of this, I fell fast asleep.

III

Towards morning it got cold in the barn, and as I pulled the blanket around me again in my half-sleep, I felt my wife's sleep-warm body against my side. I rolled over, surprised not to be able to find her breast, and found myself looking into the eyes of a child staring at me in horror.

I made some remark or other to break the spell. The merest dab of a new word is enough to make the ideas in these heads immediately fall into new patterns.

It was quite a shock to me, for these children possess the inhuman qualities of their elders; this turning to stone when you brush forbidden territory, in those horrified eyes you are guilty, and not only of touching—of other things, unspecified, much worse.

That morning, because of all the excitement, I had no bowel movement (I had merely spent a symbolic period of time on the seat in order not to appear different from the others), and accordingly I was very unhappy again. I thought I overheard the boys objecting to the wash cubicle which I had partitioned off for myself in the corner of the barn. I need this last refuge of privacy. We cannot blatantly expose our private habits; if we did, we would not be able to hold our own; and Carlton's forbearance towards me, for example, is useless when others find out that we do not wash regularly in this cold weather, or that we do not share other people's inclinations and prefer to follow our own tastes. In this bickering which accompanies my early-morning bodily discomfort, the will is deeply involved. It plays the role of a policeman who hands over the offender to the crowd that wants to lynch him. I was pursued by the vision of a pupil of the graduating class slapping my face while the class howled their approval. I was brooding over this fictitious case—the foam, so to speak, on a restless ocean—when Neumann arrived.

I saw Neumann while I was out for my morning walk, as he turned in from the road, and I tried to head him off to keep him from entering our camp, because of the danger that the boys might overhear us. But he had such a mental picture of the barn as his goal (probably from some way off, possibly even when he started out on his journey) that it was impossible to stop him, nor did he want to talk to me, except for the brief greeting which, as I walked along beside him with my much shorter steps, I did not find as unfriendly as I had expected. But for various reasons this impression was not reliable, partly because he made it clear, by the way he strode silently along, that he would not be 'available' till he got to the barn, that he regarded this unscheduled meeting as merely incidental. It must have required an extreme degree of organization to locate us. He had made up his mind to find us even before his termite march began, a march which could only be performed if performed without thinking. Fortunately, N. was exhausted by the ordeal.

A train he took to a nearby point was attacked and set on fire by fighter bombers (as one says of a general: three horses were shot from under him).

I had stored the greater part of my will elsewhere. I was in fact not prepared to give in to Neumann. He blamed me for not turning up at the agreed rendezvous. However, after speaking to me as a human being on the day of the air raid, he could not now show the contempt with which he had treated me after my dismissal. Neumann is a lean, suntanned man, the skin of his face and neck crisscrossed with lines which form hard stiff creases, which must mean there is fat beneath the skin, for that cannot be muscle; but it is a very disciplined fat, not what you might call dreamer's fat. I always claim I can see what my wife is thinking: she thinks with her shoulders, her arms, her whole body. N. doesn't do that. He uses the logic springing from his head to riddle his environment, but he does not really grasp it. My incompetence he could forgive; but that I was opposed on principle to leaving this place was something he could not understand. I tried to divert his attention by talking about what was likely to happen on the Oder and Rhine fronts. He had to admit that the Oder front had probably already collapsed. He tried to brush away this conversation, which I had spread over him like a net, but the subject was well chosen. Again and again I find it is the magic of words which is my best weapon, a weapon which does not fail me even with someone like N., who is only partially susceptible, but I wouldn't be able to ensnare him in symbols. After a time, when I felt equal to it again, I resumed the conversation about our evacuation. I took as my main argument the fact that, for the time being, we were safe here. N. had to admit that the boys assembled at the rendezvous had already been listed in the rolls, that their camp was known to all the authorities, and in all probability they would be recruited for defence purposes. I enumerated many other reasons for my standpoint, perhaps not quite as convincing. I could not give in, if only because, even if I gave in now, it would still mean a severe punishment and a denunciation by N. Like Wallenstein, I had already gone too far, in a kind of intoxication with my victory over this man who had made my life a misery for four years and now proved incompetent in a simple dialogue. I cited the case of my grandfather who, when his strength for all else failed, took to breeding sheep. He lived for the sheep, he mashed potatoes for the sheep, cut the bad places out of the potatoes before feeding the sheep, later he slaughtered the sheep. Also: that we had to cultivate the boys like valuable trees—a rare plant—and must not expose them to destruction, for every boy is unique, even though they tend to look alike. It was really the incompetence of the teachers that made them look alike. He wouldn't admit this. I attacked him at another point: in Dresden, after Luther's death, the traditional exorcism of the Devil at baptism was to be abolished. A butcher stood behind the priest and threatened to bring his axe down on him if he did not drive the Devil out of his infant son. Neumann did not think this proved anything, since reason ultimately opposed driving out the Devil. Not when the butcher is standing behind you, I replied. Carlton still did not turn up. I sent someone to look for him. Right to the end, I believed the decision would be made on the field of argument. But N. had got an idea into his head: he had decided I didn't want to join the last-ditch stand. I got Carlton to drive him to the station, which was several miles away, and gave him a bottle of cognac as a parting gift, although I could certainly have put it to better use than he could, for he will only give it away.

I wandered around some more for a while, the conversation had made me restless. Now that I can do so without jeopardizing the issue, I find Neumann's attitude admirable. My thoughts seldom fit what I want to say. Like the Polish miners' families, who multiply to such an extent during the long journey from their native country to the Rhineland that the houses which have been prepared for them are no longer big enough, my similes are no longer big enough for my rapidly multiplying thoughts, although only a moment ago they were. Respect for humanity and scholarship prevents people like Carlton or N. from casually knocking over the frail thought-structures we are able to offer them. They are not really thought-structures, they are secret symbols which sound like nonsense, I am now about to give another simile: they are the echo-sounding devices I need in order to plumb my real meaning.

My Dearest,

I hope you're not getting into too much mischief in Karlsbad. I don't say this because you're my wife, for in these troubled times such an attitude is pretty irrelevant. Nor do

I wish to dress up in biological disguise something which is morally obsolete: that it would be better for your health, for instance, and for your complexion, if you exercised some restraint. Oh well, there's really no point in my telling you all this. The distance between us is more than I can bear. The alleged dangers which threaten you and which my jealousy invents are gigantic. Why did you have to go to that wretched Karlsbad again? Haven't I warned you that your lust for life is bound to drive you to disaster? With life as complicated as it is for us all nowadays, you can't simply start living and think everything's going to be all right. I don't mean to say Nature is our enemy, but I believe that you in your way have just as little notion of how to get along with yourself as I have in mine. You can't run wide-eyed to meet your happiness. Be careful how you pick your adventures. But what am I worrying about, maybe you really are only taking the cure, though I find that hard to imagine!

When we went to the station, the two of us, and we were at a loss for words before we said goodbye, we had both stopped talking, wasn't our quarrel over by then? How often have we quarrelled like that, and our tears were the beginning of an embrace! Wasn't everything all right again as we sat in the station restaurant with our farewell drinks? I can't believe those were the final words of our marriage, just because you might be silly enough to rush headlong into disaster. You only have to make friends with one of those big brutes who are probably lying around in Karlsbad, convalescing and watching their end approach, one way or another. You leave your hotel in the morning, walk through the park. The eyes of the less seriously wounded follow you from countless hotel windows. In the evening, you are simply incapable of resisting the words and hints, the pleas. Your imagination is highly inflammable, and you are too much alive to offer any resistance. You become hopelessly involved, your head full of hopes of something undefined, something for which in this way it is surely too late now. The Czechs watch you and will include you in their revenge. What are you hoping for? What have you been looking for all these war years? You know as well as I do that you never find anything in these little adventures. I believe we are all in the grip of that solemn feeling which this war has spread among us, a deceptive feeling which seems to bring our ideals within our reach. Must something even greater emerge when the great soap bubble of war bursts? Why didn't you stay with me? I didn't want to persuade you not to go because I was hoping that in a moment of magnanimity you would say: Should I stay, or should I go? Let the train go without me, you might have said. But the noise inside you, your lack of confidence in me, your doubts as to whether I am still your ideal or one of your disappointments which you shed like a dress that hasn't brought you any luck! And yet maybe you want to spare your ideal, give me a respite till I've got hold of myself again?

How often have your Don Juans in Karlsbad, whom I envy and hate, disappointed you when they have tried out their newly won life-force on you? But do you shed them? Dutifully you carry your beautiful sensuality year after year to market. If you were here, and I could hold you in my arms, I would not be so suspicious. You are too good-natured, too optimistic, much too unsuspecting—even though you suspect me. You are fooled, you think there are people who know you as I know you. When you are

> looking for something difficult to learn, when you are looking for something new which might work a miracle, when you press yourself against me and caress me because you would like to find out more about miracles. Ambitious and corruptible through your skin, but also incorruptible through your skin, which never forgets a disappointment. I can't stand our being so far apart, otherwise I wouldn't be writing all this; if I could only touch you, I would know you are safe. The men you are going around with now will exploit you and pass you on from one to the other. And when the Russians arrive, you will be surprised because those same men will trade you for food or a bicycle. I know I'm talking nonsense, but I can't stand our being so far apart, it seems unnatural. Why didn't you stay with me? A streak of generosity, the kind you admire in yourself, just one second, enough for you to say: Well, should I stay?

This letter, like a number of others, could not, of course, be mailed by Schincke where he was. He hesitated to give the letter to Neumann, who might have been able to mail it somewhere; besides, when Neumann turned up the letter was still only a torso. And he had no intention of asking Carlton to mail it, although Carlton might have found an opportunity. Moreover, it was doubtful whether the mail was still getting through to Karlsbad. Nor was Schincke sure how his wife would react to this letter, he knew what she was thinking when he could look at her, but he was helpless when he knew she was far away. So Schincke left the letter among his papers which were gradually accumulating here.

IV

Carlton told me there is a big estate near by. It is situated in the hills we can see from the barn. Next to the manor house are the houses for the farm labourers, two great wings built of brick, next to them the huts for the Polish women labourers and the Russian prisoners. Carlton has made contact with the people who run the estate. He maintains he knows the lady of the manor, but I regard this as an attempt to impress me. To make his conquest sound more believable, he says he has ceased to find any pleasure in her. (But he has found out, so he says, that he can use her for our purposes, and that makes up for it. He doesn't have to love her, he says, he just has to get something out of it.)

He has brought me two volumes of Montaigne bound in red morocco. I had hinted he might take a look in the toilets, reading matter was often left lying around there. Now he has brought along these dark-red beauties, they made their appearance just as I was emerging, invigorated, from my midday nap: the most receptive moment of the day. I wanted to kiss him on the lips, but it misfired because he tried to shake me off. He allows me to do many unusual things. Moreover, he has brought me a list of all the members of the First Infantry Guard Regiment for the years 1904 and 1905. Now I can pore over all those glorious names.

The children are being taken to the manor house for a bath. This has to be done at night, of course. I have prepared myself for this nocturnal adventure by an invigorating sleep, for which I lay down after sunset. This sleep before a party or a tour of the dance halls and night clubs: you wake up with lips so full of blood you could cut right into them and the crimson blood would come spurting out in a great arc. Your body feels like a mere husk for this pulsating blood, like the skin of a balloon. I took my turgid lips like an engorged coxcomb to Carlton, who was just about to start up the truck, but there seemed to be some hitch. I was instantly seized with that old fear that the adventure might not take place; a reflex which has always prevented me from running any risk before a party or an adventure, whether it was putting on any clothes except the ones I can count on to always bring me luck, or asking Carlton why he couldn't get the truck started by kicking it, as I had seen him do before, I simply can't think why I didn't love this reliable beast right from the beginning, with its great headlights up front, although they are only visible through narrow slits. It is much easier to control than horses, which have always seemed uncanny to me with their housewives' eyes. You can't get as fond of them as you can of this machine when it starts rattling after a few bangs and kicks. The headlights are turned on, Carlton happens to touch the horn, and the truck makes a sound like a dog that interprets even its master's involuntary movements as orders.

For some reason or other, I had expected us to be received at the estate with hurricane lamps, but then of course we would not have had to come at night. I am inclined to regard caution as a refinement of pleasure, and was surprised when I found myself actually in danger here, for Carlton hissed at me when I got out and was about to speak to the boys. Lights were still burning in the servants' quarters, so we had to stop the noisy truck some distance from the main house, unload our freight quietly and take it to a rear entrance, where a maid was waiting for us.

Here I was, like in the campaign in France. I found my way to the manor's panelled library. Carlton tried to usher me out of there, because he said it might be dangerous if lights were seen. I must admit I had turned them all on as if for a party (the mistress of the house ought to consider Carlton sufficient recompense for the increase in the light bill). However, I was able to point out that the blinds were drawn and that the owner could suddenly decide she wanted something to read just as easily as I. I still believed Carlton really did know the owner, for which reason a good deal was permitted which would otherwise not be so in a stranger's house. Carlton, who knew better but who was easygoing by nature, gave in and left me in the library.

I had already picked out several books and arranged them around me. So there I was, sitting among my treasures, when the mistress of the house walked in. I rose courteously and, as one does when getting up from one's chair to greet a visitor, a little stiffly. I kissed her hand and introduced myself a little stiffly too. I alluded to my friend Carlton, but she did not react to this, which meant that I spoke several sentences into a void. But it was not out of the question for me to get this woman to like me, since Carlton, as I well knew, had arrived at such-and-such a point. She offered me some cognac. I also accepted a cigarette. She held hers with a charming gesture slightly away from herself while she poured the cognac. She seemed to be surprised at our visit rather than prepared for it. We had reached the vicinity of the cognac again before it became evident that she had not invited us at all.

Despite all my democratic ideals—and the important thing after all is to see that the masses share in our cultural heritage, and failure to solve the problem of the masses is the thing I blame National Socialism for in my heart of hearts—whenever I find myself with people of my own kind, i.e. members of the elite—and how much more does this apply in lonely rural surroundings!—I am overwhelmed by happiness, a sense of belonging, which I would not care to be deprived of and which I would strive to salvage in a new era, if such salvaging were possible (and there were a new era). Among equals everything is permissible: the old game of pretence, the fluctuation between the highest breeding and animal bodies; I know that is all out of date and bad, but for an hour it held me spellbound again. This woman, whose husband was in command of a regiment somewhere in Croatia, even supposing he were still alive, this woman who offered me cognac that got under my skin and spread warmth inside me while her words were warming me outside, gave me books, at least she said I could take along any of the books I had chosen. It is only natural that I felt like an officer in enemy country, since the mood of this conversation matched the age of bygone wars.

V

The high-pitched humming of the little motor approaching from the road, like a bloodthirsty insect. Sensing danger when the sound suddenly ceased, I had gone out to our sentry. On the way, I suddenly saw the farmer, as if he had shot up out of the ground, this is the order in which I received my impression of him: old green hat, clumping boots, little brown eyes, an armband.

'Heil 'tler.'

'Heil Hitler,' I replied and invited him to come along for a drink: 'Let's have a drink first, shall we?' The farmer demanded to see my papers. I did not understand right away what he wanted, and these moments were wasted for my deliberations, since he took my failure to understand for evasion. I gave him what I had on me: pension card, monthly streetcar pass with photo. In the interval that followed, while the farmer studied the documents, I said we had been bombed out and ordered to come here. Some boys came running up, and I sent a few of them to get Carlton. The farmer looked up puzzled from his papers.

'You don't seem to have any proper identification,' he said, handing me back the papers. He asked me some more questions, and I was glad about this, for it seemed to me that if we could only talk long enough, I was bound to be able to unthaw him. I wanted to show him everything. I did not leave my farmer's side for an instant, I kept on talking to him in persuasive tones, the way my wife has heard me do whenever I am involved with the police or anything really dangerous. I laid mines, so to speak, I produced so many reasons why it was lawful and necessary for us to remain here that if he tried to get his thoughts back on the old track they were bound to step on these mines and be thrown off the track. I had the feeling we might be able to win the farmer round. The farmer said: 'Please order all the members of your party to assemble here.'

'And what's going to happen to the children?'

He did not answer; instead he sat down by my table. Apart from turning his thick skull a couple of inches, he gave no sign of life. I once heard of a farmer who lost his way in his fields when he was drunk, and, because he persisted with his drinking movements, swallowed so much earth that he died. I saw Carlton, the boys. The sense of gratitude and the fresh wave of assurance when I saw them come in. It was the same deceptive feeling of security as I had that time when I opened the front door and the four Brownshirts approached and I saw the taxi driver turn his cab round and come back again so that the Brownshirts stopped approaching. But just as the taxi driver, in spite of some shouting back and forth with the Brownshirts, could not protect me, and one of the Storm Troopers managed to get his foot in the door and nab me in the hall, so Carlton's protection failed me here too.

'I've been arrested, Carlton,' I called out to him. 'The children are being taken away!'

But by now the farmer had come to life, he went over to Carlton and did the same as he had with me.

'Your identity papers, please,' etc.

All the boys had arrived by this time, the farmer ordered them to form ranks of three and, since he did not trust me and Carlton, put the boys Pichota and Hartmann in command. They immediately set about dividing up the boys. I had the terrible feeling that everything was slipping through my fingers.

'What's going to happen to the children?' I asked again, and in such a loud voice that the farmer looked round. Carlton did nothing. The organizing of the boys took some time. I tried to catch

Hartmann's and Pichota's eyes, but they avoided mine, they obeyed the one who had entrusted them with this important responsibility. Only a few of the smaller boys seemed to have kept a natural sense of what was right and proper. I tried to communicate with them by signs. They looked at me uncertainly, not knowing what to make of them. Then a few of the boys who had not yet been split up into ranks ran out towards the road. The farmer, not grasping what was happening but sensing danger, drew his pistol and shouted: 'Stop!' But he could not shoot because we were on top of him. The boys' ranks broke up.

When we got off him (like dogs who have got their teeth into an enemy dog), he stood up, his green hat rather battered, a gaping wound in his face. Without a word, he walked over to his motorbike, blood dripping, spattering his jacket, while we stayed right where we were so as not to undermine our victory. He picked up his bike, an ordinary bicycle to which he had attached an auxiliary motor, and pushed it towards the road, walking like a man who is retreating but doesn't want to show he has cause to retreat. For quite a while we could hear the malevolent throbbing of the auxiliary motor driving his bike up the hill.

VI

Towards evening, armoured vehicles and army transport trucks appeared on the road going past our hideout, three abreast and pulling cannons, they were making for the hills. Their headlights were switched off, the only sounds were the deep roar and the clanking of treads from the road. After a time, the column came to a standstill, orders were shouted, some vehicles tried to move on by pulling out sideways across the field. Perhaps they were afraid that fighter planes might recognize the vehicles in the dusk with night binoculars? Presently a military staff gathered round an officer a little way off the road, and dispatch riders were sent out from this command post.

On my evening walk, accompanied by some of the boys, I went as far as the convoy. From one of the officers' cars came the sound of music. I could not identify it right away. I told the boys who were with me to listen closely, and spoke sharply to them when they gave no immediate sign of listening, the way one speaks sharply to someone who refuses a piece of bread in times of dire shortage. There is nothing more annoying than a lack of intuitive awareness.

The musical presence which had brought me happiness here in my exile in the country (rather like being exiled to the Black Sea) lasted only a moment. The driver of the vehicle, who had been talking to the other drivers, came over to us. I tried to head him off as he approached the car and make him realize the beauty of the music before he could turn it off. He looked up in surprise from his wordless trot. He walked round me, as I was standing in his way. I was therefore several paces away from the vehicle and could not prevent him from reaching inside. I said: 'Please don't turn off the music for a moment,' etc., but he had already found another station. The soldier remained standing near us but looked over at us with a not-unfriendly expression.

VII

Yesterday we could hear cannons booming from the west during the day. Some of the vehicles on the road tried to reach the hills but were discovered by fighter planes. Carlton has been gone for two days. He is full of projects, restless as a gambler, a threat to our safety. Nevertheless, I looked for him, towards the road—until I thought, he won't come if I keep looking. So I went back, feeling certain he had already returned to the barn, but I did not find him there.

I have sent out search parties to look for Carlton.

Carlton has been hanged. From the curving bough of a pine tree. Chalk marks on the soles of his shoes, like the ones foresters make on trees.

I have been to see the lady of the manor because I have to talk to someone. But she received me with such exceptional warmth that I soon found myself in a false situation. I kept on chatting, not knowing how to break out of this diabolical circle. From my full heart, as if from a full stomach, I suggested we call each other by first names. The sudden intimacy brought my emotions to the surface and I could have talked about Carlton's black tongue, but just then she made some witty remark, I don't remember now what it was—temporary mental anaesthesia brought on by the joke—the result was we lapsed again into a warm, unreal tone of voice, as if we were saying goodbye while we finished our drinks, until she let me out into the night, and then she could not refrain from saying my first name, which had been on the tip of her tongue: Eberhard.

VIII

Shoals of silver fish with bloody heads: all day long, they fly back and forth over the road. Not a vehicle escapes their notice. I am completely out of touch with the situation. I find all this terribly exciting although I ought really to see the danger. But I quite like the danger, I ought really to be worrying about my safety and that of my pupils, but all I want to do is start teaching again.

Dream No. 1

I have been dancing all night with a very short hunchbacked man, I have to bend right down to him, he is wearing riding breeches. Feel a great revulsion, but am afraid that to refuse him would be harmful to me.

Dead mouth, drawn tightly together like a miser's purse (André Gide). All day long, I have been fluctuating between two quotations which are meaningless to me but which I can't get out of my head:

> Appropinquante morte animus multo est divinior (Cicero, *De Divinatione*, I, 63).
>
> A man sentenced to death says: Light! An immense quantity of light, thanks be to God! Another man turns his food bowl upside down over his head and says: Let's go! We must play the fool to the very end.

Dream No. 2

Practice alert! We are taken out onto an open square where a guillotine has been erected. We are told this is merely a trial run to establish the height of our necks so that, in the event of an execution, we could be correctly laid out on the plank and the procedure carried out more quickly. In place of the guillotine blade, a typewriter ribbon has been stretched across the frame. The whole thing looks like a fretsaw, only that instead of the saw blade there is a typewriter ribbon, and when it drops it will mark the exact point of impact. They stand us up there in turn. I don't trust it at all, I suspect they're going to secretly exchange the ribbon for a blade. I have just been fastened into position when I look up. And there I see, the shining blade of an axe. I scream: 'There!'

IX

In the case of the farmer, at least I was immediately aware of his malevolence. I am not cut out for situations like this. I am really no more restless than at any other time, probably I lack a proper grasp of the situation, but what am I supposed to do? Perhaps I used to have the necessary fear, distributed through my life to date? I could not claim to be exercising my mind since there has been this danger. One ought to be able to use one's brain now, but I cannot really relate to danger. What use is my head to me now if they can bash it in at any moment? It must be better protected; we can divide up the human mind into an efficiently working brain, like Carlton's, although this didn't help him, and measures for protecting that brain. But how am I to explain this to someone who believes in the power of the intellect? Hanging from that tree, and his tongue! Not a thing one can do, not a thing; like two logs, those legs. I could have touched them. Would never have dared do such a thing when he was alive. But seeing him hanging there like that, it's really impossible to think why I didn't. Maybe we had better leave?

I came on the officer unawares while he was talking to the boys. As I approach, silence on the part of the boys and the officer, as if I had surprised a pair of lovers. I asked the officer if I could speak privately to him, regardless of whatever he wanted with the boys. He tried to make excuses and did not want to follow me into the barn, but after my short midday nap I was like a recharged battery. My suspicion that he wanted to talk the boys into joining a trench-digging detail proved to be correct. I showed him the weapon I had taken from the farmer. There were no vehicles to be seen on the road at this time.

I allowed him to pick up the bicycle on which he had ridden here and wheel it to the road. He was no coward. As he rode off, I fired a bullet after him which crashed into the trees lining the highway.

Guards have been posted while we start to work. The guards keep us informed about the traffic on the highway. The meaning of the last few days cannot be: live dangerously; if only because there is the possibility that we shall not survive the danger. I break off, the guards signal. The sound of engines comes up the road.

X

Et volat saepius carta caritatis alis pennata implens officium linguae.

78:119,25

In a letter to Theodulf of Orléans, Alcuin gives the following definition: *memor esto sacerdotalis dignitatis linguam caelestis esse clavem imperii et clarissimam Christi tubam. Quapropter ne sileas, ne taceas, ne formides loqui.*

225:368,29

Loqui is therefore a spiritual duty and corresponds to priestly dignity. Respect for the word involves obligation towards the word on the part of the priest. Hence the recurrent admonition to speak: *nolite tacere.*

225:413,4

Silentium in sacerdote pernicies est populi. Loqui is justified not as an arbitrary communication but by its inherent goal: it is the key to *imperium regni caelestis.*

113:164,32

Rationalis intellegentia is the organ in which *discere* has its seat and at which *docere* is aimed. It is the natural property of man. Mention has already been made of the qualifying *rationalis* in Alcuin.

113:164,34

Lingua: seat of *loqui* and thus of *docere*, implies *rationalis intellegentia*; *cor* on the other hand is the organ of reception of *gratia*, the seat of *religio*. In *cor* and *intellegentia* we have a further example of those dual unities which so frequently mark style and thought of the sources of that time.

Sapientia forms a kind of synthesis of *intellegentia* and *cor*. It is *sapientia* which triumphs over the state of *rudis* as it has been adopted as a term from the works of St Augustine (i.e. as *catechizandus*), and as it is understood in the circumstances and conditions of the eighth century.

34:75,24

Alcuin is concerned for the welfare of his pupils and does all he can for them. In a letter to Adalhard of Corbie, he begs him to intercede with Charlemagne to permit his pupil Bernarius to return from the world to his monastery *Lérins*.

There is a further example of a dispute on behalf of pupils. in this case, however, with a more 'official' background and more serious consequences. It leads to a temporary breach between Alcuin and Theodulf of Orleans, and even to a severe reprimand from Emperor Charlemagne.

During the day, Schincke was at work again on his paper on the cultural reforms of the Carolingian empire, which he had started planning in 1932 and writing in 1934. He realized that, like resuming teaching, this could be an inappropriate reaction to events and the present situation; but what reaction was to be expected from him? The very fact that it was an emergency made him cling instinctively to what he knew. What else could he have done? Plot a revolution? He sensed that the turning point he had been waiting for since 1933 was now past, and that this time there had been no change either. He was glad to be able to safeguard the remnant of good will which he still possessed by investing it here in literary productivity. Instinctively, he moved towards this opportunity: to make a new beginning with the boys in his care. The following day, after being denounced by the farmer whom he had wounded and who came from a nearby village, Schincke was arrested by a mobile military court. The boys were rounded up and taken to neighbouring farms. Schincke was taken to the nearest large town. It was while he was there, separated from his pupils, that he was liberated.

Film stills from *Abschied von Gestern* (Yesterday Girl). The film focuses on the story of Anita G. It premiered at the 1966 Venice International Film Festival, and received the first Silver Lion award for a German film since 1940.

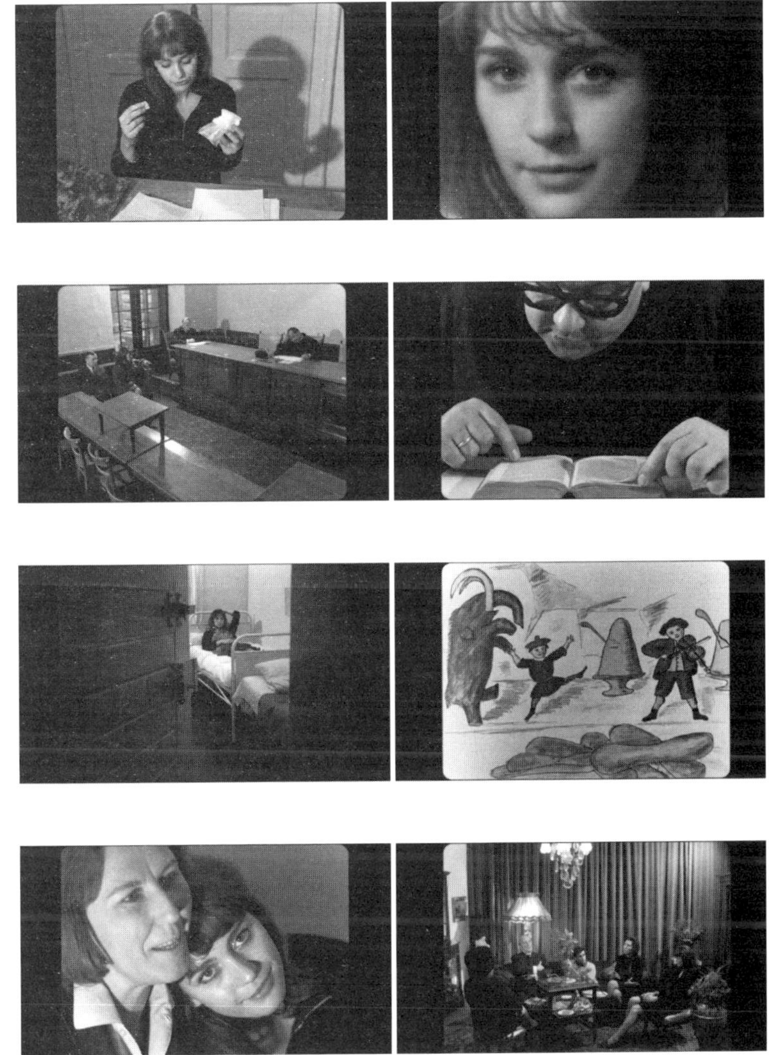

FIGURE 2
The leading role of Anita G. in *Abschied von gestern* (Yesterday Girl) was performed by my sister Alexandra Kluge.

ANITA G.

Don't you know a more cheerful story?

II

The girl Anita G., crouching under the staircase, saw the boots when her grandparents were taken away. After the capitulation, her parents returned from Theresienstadt, something no one would have believed possible, and founded factories in the vicinity of Leipzig. The girl attended school, looked forward to a normal life. Suddenly she became frightened and fled to the Western zones. Of course she committed thefts. The judge, seriously concerned about her, gave her four months. She only served two, the rest she spent on probation in the care of a probation officer. That woman was overzealous in her duties—the girl fled to Wiesbaden. From Wiesbaden, where she found peace and quiet, to Karlsruhe, where she was pursued, to Fulda, where she was pursued, to Kassel, where she was not pursued, to Frankfurt. She was apprehended and (there being a warrant out for breach of probation) transferred to Hanover. She escaped to Mainz.

Why does she constantly infringe on private property as she travels? She appears under a variety of names in various police departments' all-points bulletins. Why doesn't this intelligent person regulate her affairs in a satisfactory manner? She moves from one rooming house to another, mostly she has no room at all because she quarrels with the landladies. One can't drift around the country like a gypsy. Why doesn't she behave sensibly? Why doesn't she stay with the man who is making a play for her? Why doesn't she face facts? Doesn't she want to?

II

She took the man she had met the previous day up to the room that was no longer hers. Here, this way, she whispered, hearing him grope cautiously behind her in the dark. He could not move without making some sound. He was not very adept anyway. She moved towards him in the darkness, and, taking him by the hand, led him past her former landlady's quarters to her own room. She locked the door and switched on the light.

The man disapproved of all this fuss, but did not know the reason for it. He probably thought she was anxious not to disturb the relatives with whom she was staying. He would have preferred to call on these relatives and regularize his new contact with this attractive girl. He was not one for secrets. In fact he told her so. But she didn't want to explain to him just then why the room was no longer hers. Frau Schepp's reasons for evicting her, or why she had given up the room of her own accord and thereupon been evicted by Frau Schepp, couldn't be explained in a few words. Frau Schepp: large, unusual hat, large eyes full of little vanities and a hard sparkle. Her husband, at least that's what some people say, flung himself off the third-floor balcony while she was busy in the next room. Maybe Frau Schepp counted on the girl sneaking back in? The girl moved about the room without making a sound, which for her was easier than being noisy; she was one of those people who lack the imagination to make noise. The man bumped into the iron bedstead. She trembled at the thought of Frau Schepp.

The warmth and security emitted by the body lying beside her did not reassure A. The pale, coarse skin, the close-set nipples, surrounded by long fine hairs, seemed themselves in need of protection. She had none to give. If it did not concern her in some important aspects, she might even find this man ridiculous—his anxieties, his fear of embarking on something illicit. She lacked the ability to take her time and select the people she really wanted to be with. Impatiently, she accepted anyone prepared to take an interest in her. It was a chance to restore her life to a state of security and order. That was why she wanted to preserve her advantage.

She felt chilly in the unheated room, and the prospect of the cold she would come down with was both enjoyable and unwelcome, because it would be a nuisance, something like having a baby—she sought the warmth in the body lying beside her which she had to get used to all over again. She was not shy with him now. She let him have any part of her body he wanted. She gave herself with a simplicity that even simple people do not possess, and took care that what she narrated of her past sounded natural. She arranged her past in such a way that it could not upset him. She made no plans, she merely waited for his suggestions for the next day. Touching the thin quilt, she reassured herself that the body was still sleeping beside her. While he was there, she slept outside the quilt, at the edge of the bed, on her side and leaning lightly against the pile under the quilt; she was afraid that otherwise she might disturb him with her movements which she could not control during the night.

Towards morning the man woke up and turned to her again. She would have liked to spare him this exertion because under no circumstances did she want him to do more than he wanted to do himself. She did not want this night, which might be the last, to leave a bad taste in his memory. On the other hand, she could not very well deny him if she wished to be simple and natural. She made an effort to appear interested, but was not very successful. She was so anxious to know what he would say that she missed what he said to her. She pulled the quilt up over the exhausted man and reproached herself for not having been of use to him. She nestled up to the quilt and waited till he had fallen asleep. Whatever happened, she did not want to take advantage of him. Most of all, she did not want to take advantage of him in this particular way, which was of no benefit to her.

She could not move without making a sound, nor silently open each lock. The man stumbled as she let him out, but this merged with the morning noises of the house. It broke her heart to watch him dress in the chilly room, but there was nothing she could do about it since she was not even supposed to use the room. She let him go quickly, so that these moments would not be etched in his memory. As soon as he had gone, she left the apartment as well.

II

She wanted to see him once more before she left town. For many weeks she had been prolonging this relationship from day to day, although her situation in the city was becoming increasingly dangerous. She went to look for him and after a time found him in the cafe opposite the cathedral. He still looked tired, slack-mouthed and hollow, drawn-in, 'frosted' lips. A rather trite conversation. To a man sitting next to him: He had been on night shift . . . , when you go to bed with a passionate woman. . . . He was not aware of her nearness.

She was taken aback. So this was all that love accomplished. She wished she had left the day before. No matter how much of her strength she invested in this man, he remained a blank. She despaired of his ever being useful to her. She accompanied him at a distance to the government offices into which, as was his daily habit, he disappeared. Later, she calmed down. She decided to give it one more try.

IV

The Background Can Be Sketched in Briefly

She would never have exchanged one word with this man if the accident had not brought them together. On the day in question in May 1956, A. wanted to leave Mainz because she had got into debt at a number of rooming houses near the railway station, and for various other reasons no longer felt safe in the city. Before leaving the city, she visited the university, which was situated on a rise. She passed the day sitting in the university lounges and attending lectures. She wanted to go to Wiesbaden and possibly get a job there, but at the university gates, as she was crossing the street, she was struck by a car (she may also have walked into it). She picked herself up and examined the abrasions. The car owner walked up to her and slapped her. She did not know how to react. Later, she got to know the man better. Had it not been for the accident, she would never have talked to him at all. The man encouraged her to remain in Mainz, to look for a job and a place to live. He was anxious she have enough money and a job. He was afraid that otherwise her inactivity might prove an obligation. Although he categorically rejected any kind of obligation, he failed, during the subsequent course of this relationship, to exercise the proper caution. She noted the consequences of his carelessness but kept this fact to herself, probably because she was afraid of his reaction; besides, he did not ask about it.

V

Looking for an Attorney

Her attention had been drawn to a newspaper article describing the career of a Frankfurt attorney, Mr Sch. She went to Frankfurt and tried to get in touch with this defence counsel. But he could not be reached at his office all morning. In the afternoon, she saw him from a distance at the courthouse, the attorney's head clerk having advised her to look for him there. She did not dare speak to him when, surrounded by a covey of questioners, he left the courtroom and descended the wide staircase. Later that afternoon, he was still not available whenever she phoned his office. She did not want to make an appointment for one of the following days, she had already given up hope of being able to see the famous man and interesting him in her case. She refused to talk to one of his junior associates because she had confidence only in the counsellor himself; besides, she believed that only he could dispense advice free of charge. Her mistake was that at the very beginning—the first time she phoned, in fact—she had been too diffident. That explained why the office staff had given her the brush-off.

The Counsellor's Day

The famous man spent the morning wandering about his apartment in his dressing gown. He was not curious about the new day. He telephoned Wiesbaden and Zürich and then sat down at his desk.

His hand lay on the desk, resting on the second and fifth fingers, thumb quietly at the side, third and fourth fingers kneeling. As he slowly raised his fourth finger and brought it forward, there came a moment when the two kneeling fingers snapped forward together and the hand fell flat on the desk. He did not answer, waited until the secretary gave up knocking and went away from the door. Thick veins on the back of his hand, which was narrow with a few hairs on it; the two kneeling fingers thrust forward and the hand lying flat, out of breath, so to speak, on the desk. He looked at it, he was not curious about the day.

Later, some associates needed his approval of an urgent decision. He took part by telephone in a discussion concerning a remission of sentence at the Department of Justice. The telephone calls stimulated him a little. If he feigned interest in these discussions long enough, he became interested. One after another, his associates phoned him and asked for his advice. He was not in the mood. A forceful person cannot be enlightened. How weak must a person be to be enlightened?

The middle part of the day ran according to a schedule which he was able to influence only by postponing his departure from one meeting or appointment to the next; his chauffeur, however, who manoeuvred him expertly through the afternoon traffic, partially recouped this lost time. His two co-counsels were waiting for him at the entrance to the courthouse. He followed them to those terrible courtrooms. The exhausting performance at lunchtime, now over, had tired him. Exhausting: because as well as wit, intelligence, astuteness—qualities which, incidentally, he did not really possess—he was obliged to display fortitude in drinking and eating; the very opposite of his talent for manoeuvring. Part of his popularity was based on these pretended qualities. He approached the accused on the stand with ambivalent emotions, spoke to various people before reaching his seat, then turned to greet the accused in the usual manner. The two co-counsels turned the pages of the briefs. He withdrew to the furthest corner of the bench to see whether there was a draught there. The accused was questioned. He was a fat, well-paying businessman brought up on a morals charge. The defence counsel stood in front of his table waiting to see if he should intervene. His movements were as stealthy as if he had to catch or measure something. He was tired, he stumbled over his words when he spoke, turning half towards the accused and half towards the judge's bench, and all the while, with subdued catlike tread, as if not to frighten away an idea of insult or hurt or alarm anybody, he paced up and down on the polished floor in front of the counsel table. He found it hard to concentrate. The judge and jury became restless. The judge did not like him. It was only his name that kept them in line. He stumbled over his words several times, and the whole performance was really not very prepossessing; during his pleadings, the judge leafed through his papers. How could he harm him?

When judgement had been handed down, attorneys and others surrounded him like a swarm of admirers and shielded him from awkward questions. The accused thanked him. In the hallway, a number of people approached who wished to speak to the counsellor. He hunched his shoulders because he was afraid of the draughts in the hallway, nevertheless he stopped to chat to some of them. That afternoon he was supposed to drive out with the district attorney to the State Mental Hospital, as he thought he had discovered a case there which necessitated the intervention of either himself or the DA. Instead, he sat for a time with the DA over tea.

This tall, well-protected man, who did not have many more years to live, made little use of his influence. He had more influence than he would admit to himself. About this hour of the evening, he began to perk up a little; in the late afternoon, he had taken drops which stimulated the heart for conversation and widened the arteries. In no respect could he be said to be a specialist, not even in his capacity as an attorney, because nowhere was he prepared to feel secure; but he had specialized insofar as all his power was concentrated on combating the pogrom that might be unleashed again at any time. This power could therefore be drawn on solely for the purpose of warding off danger. He had another five years or so to live, and for that length of time did not need to exert himself unduly. He knew enough ways of getting by. He could stay aloft, so to speak, motor idling, until he glided to the final landing, if this be a fitting comparison. That evening he went to bed early. He could still have wielded a great deal of influence, but there was nothing he wanted. He wanted to return to the womb. He did not believe in change; in fact, as long as he was not in danger, he was against change, as one never knew whether it might not be accompanied by danger.

Need for Protection

Very thin limbs under the impeccable suit, very hairy because he had needed this protection during the first minutes of his life; no one had thought at the time that he would live; his trousers are suspended from his spine and, without touching his body at any point, hang down to his slightly splayed feet.

Covering Up, Pretence

Sits in stockinged feet, although nobody knows this, well hidden by his desk, and lets his eyes light up, 'signals' when his visitor makes a remark, he has not been listening and is pretending; it is necessary for him to impress this visitor, but not essential. The visitor is one of those people with whom, although they have no power over him, he does not on any account wish to be at odds.

Hostile Nature

He hunches his shoulders, not because it is cold but because no one knows what to say to warm him up; he looks round for a draught, a justification for his craving for warmth. He is afraid of catching cold. He cannot afford any weakening to his physique. He is shielded from people but vulnerable to draughts.

Cowardice

For over an hour, the discussion, over which he was presiding, had been going completely adrift because he refused to interrupt the speakers when they wandered off the point. Finally, they were arguing at random in the order in which they rose to speak. Many were furious at the way the debate was being conducted. The best of them were annoyed and accused the chairman of not listening. As a matter of fact, he was not listening, but no one could prove that. He put up with the hostility of the good ones and refused to interrupt the speakers, what harm could the malcontents do him? On the other hand, he was afraid of reprisals on the part of those he interrupted, if he did interrupt them; anyway, that sort of thing was foreign to his nature. (Whenever his associates made suggestions, he usually said yes, although he could equally well have said no right away, because he could equally well say no the next day, no harm could have come to him on that score, and anyway as far as his safety was concerned it made no difference whether he said yes or no; but there was also the fact that he did not like saying no, and preferred saying yes first, because there was always a chance that with time the matter would straighten itself out and he would never have to say no at all. He paid his associates to make suggestions and so also paid for the right to turn the suggestions down. But he would not have liked to tum down one of their suggestions, no doubt because he was afraid of reprisals.)

Stimulation

Three-hour luncheon in a restaurant near the station, where he receives guests whom he has to impress: he flatters the new arrivals by advancing to welcome them at the door and, on the way from the entrance to the tables, making derogatory remarks about the guests already seated. After lunch, he talks about his death, but not to everyone. The guests who heard him were not sure how they should respond. The idea of his imminent death was his most powerful stimulant, and—just as with penicillin, aspirin, etc.—he used it without compunction.

Persecution, Protégé, Two Alternatives

He has developed a magnificent apparatus capable of protecting him in the event of pogroms and, of course, even more so in times of peace. But how is he to keep the sensitive apparatus going if there is no persecution? He therefore needs a powerful stimulant to keep himself going. Naturally, the most powerful stimulant would be a protégé who is really in danger. But how is the protégé to penetrate the protective circle of fame, associates, colleagues, office staff, this complicated organization, and get through to the great defence attorney himself?

VI

The Girl Spends the Night with Her Lover in Somebody Else's Car

As he had no means of knowing where to look for her when she had no room and no fixed points at which she could be found at definite times, she waited in the street in front of his apartment until he came home in the evening. She let him go into the house, not wanting to impose on him in case he had something important to do, and when he emerged onto the street again she followed him at a distance until she was sure he was only going to the theatre. She spoke to him. He was surprised and asked her what had happened. She made up some story or other. They gave the theatre ticket to someone waiting outside the theatre. She was so glad to have found him again that she admitted having no place to go. She mentioned some money she was expecting, in order to dispel his misgivings. She found an unlocked car and said they could go for a short drive and then bring it back to the same spot. He was afraid of being discovered and fined, but she counted on it being their last evening together and so dispelled any objections he intended to raise. This was a very grave mistake on her part, for he did not feel at ease again for the rest of the evening.

He had thought it all out and planned a thorough discussion with her that day about a more permanent arrangement. He could not find the tone of voice with which these words had originally sounded in his head, but even the disconnected possibilities at which he prodded and poked sent her into sheer panic. She wanted to put him off. This was the very thing she had been so painstakingly working towards the last few weeks; now the dream was joined by a flood of objections, an antipathy towards any idea of a more permanent arrangement. Her confused emotions swept across a spectrum of reactions, she did not know how to respond. She longed for a disaster from which she could extricate him. Or for some power to intervene and put an end to her flight, so that she could confess everything—not even confess: just gain time. She compared herself to a sorceress who draws a circle around the person she loves and carries the contents of the whole world into that circle. Her face was contorted. This frightened her, for love is supposed to smooth everything out. For an instant she doubted her love and detected signs of his deceiving and trying to get rid of her by the clever use of words.

It was his custom to separate everything he did with her into an official and an unofficial part, and he tried to undress her when he had finished his dissertation. She was not prepared for it, and behaved as if she did not know what he had in mind, since she did not want to forfeit the last evening in this way. She clung to the conversation they had been having and explained why she would like to be his wife. She said 'Come here' to keep him at arm's length and talked a lot of carefully controlled nonsense. He found this very agreeable: whether she talked about their future life together or tried to please him or turned his hands away—it merely confirmed him in the direction he had taken. She tried to fend him off, but had to remain simple and natural.

For a moment she speculated on what would happen if she told him everything: the child and the police, but she could not face it. She felt it would be unfair and told him nothing about either. She released herself from his embrace in the cramped car seats and crawled out of the car. It was pouring with rain. She let the water splash onto her skin. She walked up and down. She stayed outside in the downpour until he called to her from the car. She was wet, and spoiled the upholstery when she crawled in beside him again. This confused him. He wavered between the feelings of a car owner and the feeling of her wetness.

VII

She made one final attempt to unravel her situation by asking her parents to come to Bad Nauheim from Leipzig. But in the two days she spent with them, she did not manage to pry them apart. They were a closed phalanx of fear of ordeals. What she needed was separate discussions with her mother and father, but all she could get was plenary sessions. They stuck together like wet feathers, although they had never been able to stand each other and usually took every opportunity to keep apart. They were scared of being alone with their daughter for a single moment and had reached a prior understanding.

Things had gone wrong from the very start. She had wanted to freshen up in a small café, but, before she was ready, she was discovered there by her parents, who stifled every gesture with the noise they made greeting her. She did not want to hear them make this noise, she found this as repulsive as the way they ate or did or did not notice certain things. She tried to break through their united front. This was a failure, as the conversation was soon running on the familiar track: she criticized her parents, which did her no good. She told them they hated each other, and that only made them draw closer together, as they were afraid of hatred. They pointed out how harmoniously they could live together, after so many years, if the daughter would refrain from criticizing. A. wished for a disaster to sweep away the barrier that was hardening with every word. While she was still wishing this, she lost all hope of her parents ever being able to help her. She had not realized how weak they were when they functioned jointly, how very much they had weakened each other in their marriage.

The evening of the second day in Bad Nauheim, the police, who had checked the hotel register, came and arrested her. Her parents were told of the arrest by the hotel management. The following morning A. succeeded in escaping from the police station. She hurried back to the hotel, but her parents had left. They were frightened of being dragged into the affair, regardless of what it was all about. They had not left a letter, presumably because they could not agree on what to say. A. avoided the station and the autobahn since she assumed that police were on the lookout there, and finally managed to stop a car on the federal motorway to Frankfurt.

In Mainz, on a street near the station, she ran straight into Frau Schepp. She was hurrying along, her eyes seeing nothing, till she was almost on top of her; horrified, she stepped aside to cross the street, hoping she had not been noticed. She ran in front of a car which had to jam on its brakes, forcing other vehicles to swerve; a noise that had the same effect as if searchlights were focused on her. She dashed along a street, on and on till she stood in front of her lover's apartment. She waited.

They drove to Wiesbaden. She was against this expedition as she begrudged them the little time she had left. After the trail she had left in Bad Nauheim, it could only be a matter of days before the police got wind of her. She tried to make the best of this evening, but when they had been sitting for a short while at the *Valhalla* exchanging news (which filled her with impatience—

the whores' faces, the great revolving chandelier), the police arrived for a check of identity cards. She tried to persuade the washroom attendant to show her an exit. While she could see that some prostitutes were somehow or other managing to slip away, she was kept there with half-promises. The attendant probably took her for a serious offender who could bring nothing but trouble if one did as she asked. She locked herself in a toilet. She gave the attendant all the money she had. The police ordered everyone inside the toilets to push their identity cards under the doors. They started at the left. A few moments passed, then came a 'Thank you' and the scraping of feet. A. came out when ordered to and let herself be conducted to the exit, where she tore herself loose. She spent the night in the open, halfway between Wiesbaden and Mainz. She was afraid the bridges over the Rhine would be watched at night. By late afternoon, she was waiting outside her lover's apartment, to explain why she had run away. He gave her a little less than a hundred marks and advised her to head for the Ruhr area. He did not know what he ought to do. He did not want to desert her. She found this unbearable and broke off.

VIII

She took refuge in an empty villa, the people may have fled. Even the faucets had been dismantled, perhaps everything was to be torn down. She settled into the attic rooms and could have got away with it even if they had come on her unawares. The anxiety and fatigue of the evening by the time she found the shelter on her long walk through the city streets developed during the night into a pressure in her chest, pain even when she breathed, and heavy feverish limbs. Later, her whole head was affected with the grippe that has something of death about it, her eyes cold, no warmth in them, painful eyes in deep sockets, limbs prostrate, fidgety, unresponsive.

She lay here with her illness almost like a dog in the empty house. She went out only once and bought some food, not because she was hungry but because she wanted to do something to sustain life.

IX

From two o'clock on, the lights were turned off in this corner of the large restaurant because the noon-hour stream of customers was over. When she looked up and took away her hands from her eyes, which she had been covering to warm them, she was sitting in the dark, as if in an underground passage, but there were great beams above her and along the walls, holding up the room. She assumed it was raining outside, sound of cars: things were happening. While she had kept her eyes shut, almost asleep, her blood had stayed sucking at her stomach walls, now it flowed back. Everything was functioning now, head, limbs. After a while, she left the restaurant by a side exit which could be reached from the washroom and which, unlike the main entrance, was not watched by the waiters. A car drove up to the very edge of the crosswalk. She immediately assumed a defensive pose, her hands outstretched towards the car, which did then stop in time, as close to the edge of the crosswalk as it was allowed to come.

In the late autumn, A. arrived in Garmisch, where she wanted to choose the hospital in which to have her child. She reached Garmisch in one day, but that was all she could manage. The man who had driven her there and would have looked after all her expenses wanted to take her out that evening. Her nose started to bleed, and she felt nauseated. She managed to reach the washroom, where she was safe for the time being, but later she found it impossible to be nice to the man. She did not want him.

X

Flight Movements

In Bonn, she worked as secretary and cashier for a studio theatre. A policeman's voice over the phone asked to be put through to the theatre manager. The girl thought the call referred to her. She put the call through to the manager. She took 200 marks from the till and went north. She was still trembling in the train. In the First Class waiting room at Lüneburg, the only way she could get rid of a man who kept pestering her for a date because, due to a misunderstanding, he thought she was available, was to hand over her identity card to him for safekeeping. After this, she did not dare go back into the First Class waiting room; instead, she spent the night sitting up in the Second Class one. The railway police tolerated her since she could produce a valid ticket; although it is difficult to speak of tolerance when they beat up and threw out a man only slightly shabbier who did not drink up his beer when ordered to do so. The railway was fully entitled to do this. A. took the first train passing through. On her flight, she turned to Ulm, Augsburg, Düsseldorf, Siegen, at each of which she made only a brief stop, leaving behind small debts which spurred on the wave of persecution behind her, so that—if one looks at it out of context—she seemed to be deliberately provoking this wave of persecution in order to motivate her flight movements.

XI

Flight Movements

In November, she worked in Brunswick until, returning to her landlady's with the five o'clock rush, she saw police outside the house. She fled to Stuttgart.

From Stuttgart, leaving hotel bills behind, she fled to Mannheim, Koblenz, Wuppertal, avoiding Düsseldorf, from Wuppertal to Cologne, the proximity of Koblenz scared her off and she made a detour to Darmstadt.

For purposes of illicit gain, she rented a room in Darmstadt, as she had done in various other cities, pretending a willingness to pay which, strictly speaking, she did not have.

XII

Stripped

By February, she urgently needed a more permanent place for her confinement. She tried once more in the Rhineland but, since her condition was obvious to all, no one would accept her. She gave herself up to the police, after establishing that she had no papers and could positively not manage by herself. She was remanded to the prison at Dietz. There she had to paint tiny figurines, but otherwise settled down in her protected cell. When the time came for the birth, she was transferred to the prison hospital, two separate rooms. She had no confidence in the doctor because of his fibrous skin and bad breath; he was exactly like the type of hairdresser to which she did not go. She was frightened and applied to be taken back to her cell; she had found a fellow prisoner who could help her in an emergency. But the birth began before the warden's office sent a reply. She had to let this man manipulate between her legs, but there was no time. Everything went very quickly. After two days, the child was taken away and placed in an institution near Kassel. The milk was pumped off from her breasts. For a few days, still in bed, she helped sort out the evidence against her which was scattered throughout many towns. The nervous breakdown came as a surprise to everyone. She was transferred from the prison hospital to the women's ward of the university hospital, where she was treated mainly with penicillin, and, after a time, the breakdown was brought under control.

MANFRED SCHMIDT

LIST OF CHARACTERS

MS

Helena K.

K.

Police Commissioner Peiler

F. in Sydney

Aina Sp.

Bar waitress

Lastics

E. in Pilsen

A waitress

Wounded Frenchman

A carnival princess

Representative of the Treasury Department

Representative of the Food & Drug Bureau

Representative of the Patrol & Security Service

Unnamed persons

Representative of the Police

L. (on her deathbed)

A. (Christmas Eve)

Frau M.

Members of the carnival committee

Carnival participants

Waiter

I
The Carnival

Time: 6 p.m. The bells ring out over the loudspeakers through the empty halls. Loudspeakers have been installed in the large foyer and blare across the wide staircases.

1

Trucks arrive bringing cardboard walls, churning up the snow and slush.

2

The checkroom attendants settled into their small quarters. They take part in the carnival from the safe harbour of their work.

3

The watchmen of the Patrol & Security Service in their policeman-type overcoats have hermetically sealed off the building. They are still searching the basement for loopholes in the security system.

4

Green cartons of liquor are delivered and distributed to the various floors. An out-of-town company tries to smuggle in deliveries. But there are people who see to it that only green cartons are allowed in. Suddenly the huge building was lit up, outside by floodlights, inside by smaller floodlights that had been installed everywhere.

5

Police Commissioner Peiler, wearing riding breeches, hurried through the three floors of the building. His concern: possible hiding places (among the decorations, in the washrooms) in case of a police raid.

6

When the carnival premises had been sufficiently cordoned off, the general manager and his staff withdrew to the premises reserved for the organizers. Rehearsal: 120 floodlights. Difficulties arose outside the building in connection with the increasing number of vehicles now arriving.

Interview with an Executive of the Patrol & Security Service

If we wanted to, we could make it awkward for 50 per cent of those who insult our guards. Despite all precautions, some gatecrashers manage to slip through every year and join in the carnival. These ineligible persons are usually the ones who insult our staff.

They frequently enter by way of the heating conduits, or jump onto the roof from adjoining buildings, or cause a commotion at the entrance and slip in during the general confusion. Whenever there is a ruckus at one of the entrances, we assume, and rightly so, that some gatecrashers are creating a disturbance under cover of which they will sneak in. Our staff always carry arms. However, they have instructions to resort to their weapons in exceptional circumstances only. We cannot permit the necessary task of providing security to take human lives. After all, not only would we be endangering the lives of those people, although we would shoot at their feet, we would also jeopardize the safety of our officers who risk transgressing the bounds of self-defence. For cases of disturbances of the peace reported by us, the courts pass maximum sentences of three months, with or without probation; for all cases of bodily injury and threats, according to actual or potential damages. Illegal ingress through entrances not known to us is punished by the courts with detention only. We therefore usually refrain from reporting such cases and only go after those who insult our officers. The courts as well as the carnival authorities do not take our work seriously enough because they are not familiar with the difficulties involved. It is our aim, however, to perfect the capacity for compromise and firmness of our patrol and security system, and to provide proper protection despite understaffing. We have to adapt our security methods to a changing world; at the same time, we need the cooperation of the public. Many people still feel that those who slip through the patrol and security system possibly contribute to a not-inconsiderable degree to the general gaiety and are perhaps more suitable types for the carnival than those who have lawfully produced their entrance tickets. Nevertheless, we are obliged to insist on tickets being produced. If only to avoid overcrowding.

Interview with the Leading Food Chemist, Food & Drug Bureau, Ministry of Trade & Commerce

Some people seem to imagine that they can supply these organizations with all the goods they can't get rid of in the normal way of business. But these gentlemen are profoundly mistaken. As a rule, we report up to 40 per cent in affairs of this size, based on some 20 to 30 caterers. The caterers aren't always to blame either, for they have to rely on the merchandise supplied to them.

The public will buy anything, of course. They think that, when it's a carnival, they don't have to be careful, that it's a kind of holiday. I must therefore depend to a great extent on my men in the Food & Drug Bureau, who only too often meet with hostility in their work. No one likes to have their appetite ruined, and people love parties. The caterers, on the other hand, say: What are you doing with those wieners, and so on. Many caterers refuse to go on selling to my men once they realize they are government inspectors. In such cases, the only thing my men can do is seize a sample, and if the sample fails to result in a complaint, then they're really in trouble, for then the seizure was unwarranted. Even though the work of our modest bureau meets with every possible hindrance, so far it has never been quite defeated.

The main problem is that the dealers believe they can supply such functions with poor-quality merchandise. I'd hate to tell you what's in those wieners, or what the confiscated wine you see stacked up over there consists of. People become thoroughly unscrupulous the moment they have reason to believe they are no longer dealing with a critical public but with people who are out to have fun. I don't wish to imply that our bureau ought to be any bigger. This is a problem which cannot be solved by imposing controls: rather, it must be tackled in an atmosphere of freedom. However, I would like to contradict our Honourable Minister when he states that all that is necessary is to be aware of the problem. Mere thinking about it has, as far as I know, not yet made a wiener fit to eat again, if I may be allowed this metaphor. But what does matter is wholesome food in a free atmosphere. In the Food & Drug Bureau, we perform something of the work of the detective, and it might be a good idea to write a mystery story one day and, instead of setting it among criminals and detectives, write about the Food & Drug Bureau's work in the catering business.

Interview with a Representative of the Treasury Department

We walk through the gathering with watchful eyes. Many people think they are not being observed, but they are. No one wishes to spy on them, it is their private life. Nevertheless, we see what's going on. If I am not mistaken, it was Ernest Hemingway who emphasized how many facts a writer has to know if he wishes to write only one sentence (which may have nothing to do with what he knows).

We of the Treasury Department are in a similar position. For us, life consists of learning, learning, learning. What a lot a tax official must know before he can make a proper decision! I do not wish to enlarge on the difficulties in our search for facts, but I would like to take the opportunity of pointing out that we know how many people take part in the festivities and how much merchandise is consumed. We are aware of the organizers' little tricks, that they have more tickets printed than are sold. We also see through the one about merchandise consumed, i.e. that almost as much goes back to the dealers as was supplied, even though it was sold. Our method is not to compare the quantities delivered with those left over in order to check on the turnover: the trick is based on an inadequate knowledge of our procedure. We are prepared to overlook small discrepancies, but as soon as we find anything involving excise tax, we pounce. There have been cases at affairs of this kind, where contraband cigarettes and perfume have suddenly turned up and been sold!

Interview with a Representative of the Police

Carnival? To us, it is just a taxable form of entertainment in which the ticket-buying public may participate. You all know that these affairs continually present new problems for the police, which have to be dealt with by the same number of personnel. We have an eighteenth-century police force, nineteenth-century forms of entertainment and a twentieth-century public. Conflicts are bound to arise. Yet the police have shown over and over again that they know how to celebrate when celebration is called for. I need only recall the festivities in Poland and Russia during the war, at Wilkowischen, Vilna, Mariampol, Tauroggen, Kyiv, Melitopol and in the Crimea during 1941 and '42, the Sports Carnival at Kattowitz, the ones at Lemberg and Litzmannstadt in '43, the carnivals in Smolensk, and last but not least: the one in Warsaw in 1944. The stiff, old-fashioned type of policeman has given way to a progressive, forward-looking, I might almost say jolly type of police official whose helpfulness the public appreciates more and more. If I may put it this way: nowadays, he is regarded virtually as a participant like everyone else, not as the guardian of law and order but rather as part of the organization as a whole. This new image of the police official needs to be carefully nurtured, and the task of the officers supervising the carnival should be interpreted in the same way.

Title of the Carnival

The carnival was called 'Nights of Agamemnon' because the original plan called for a carnival in ancient Greek costumes (these are easy to make and would have permitted a certain degree of nudity). The costume rules were subsequently relaxed, but the name with its effective appeal was retained. The entertainment programmes were called 'Waltzes of Love' and 'Waves of the Danube'. The carnival planners had stage fright. Would the carnival get off the ground? Would the offensive be successful?

Resistance to the Carnival

Efforts to get the carnival rolling were not successful. The well-behaved crowds circulated among the giant decorations, thronging the wide staircases. Pushing their way up and down the staircases in two great opposing streams, they had been waiting expectantly for an hour. Häbel, Schleicher, Horn I, Horn II, Putermann and Beier-Müncheberg hurried along the moving column. They kept to the centre seam joining the two streams, i.e. the only places where they could make headway. A brief ripple of excitement when some stacks of beer cases collapsed somewhere upstairs; animated motion. An exchange of words, but this is not enough to create a different climate.

Should the carnival committee have more stacks of beer cases collapse, so as to relax the atmosphere?

First Floor (Lower Beer Hall)

If only everyone were permitted to undress, oh to take off these Greek sheets, loosen ties and collars, or at least shout Nazi songs (which is prohibited)! Instead: dutifully empty the huge beer glasses.

Second Floor (Ballrooms, Bar, Wine Only)

Gitta and her friends at the table: she took off her jacket and placed her large hands on the sugar bowl, looked down her arms to see if everything was as it should be, whether her hands were placed as they should be: most of all—yes, a horse. I see them like a horse. I see something on wheels, a frame with two wheels underneath. Two little pointed feet, the legs moving like this (she demonstrates), and there's the heel . . . Gitta's remarks trailed off. No one expected a miracle from this carnival. The crowds milled about, like Christmas shoppers, through the rooms where wine only was permitted.

Third Floor (Upper Beer Hall)

Here there were groups who took offence if people tried to keep to themselves. A girl swallowed some beer from a glass, leaving white foam on her upper lip. She ran her tongue over her lips to wipe them clean; thereupon she was jeered at by people at the next table. At the counter, F. let a home economist embrace him, there was such a draught that this was the only way to survive the evening without catching cold. When P. knocked at the door of a toilet, his girl came out with an escort. What is one to do with a girl who says: I feel like eating ice cream till they gas me?

Tending the Carnival, 1

At last the fanfare, scheduled for 8.30, announcing the programme 'Waltzes of Love'. Instructions to start ahead of time came from the management. Brintzinger and Karlota conveyed the instructions. In fact, the programme began at once in all the halls but failed to catch on because the crowds kept circulating. All the programme achieved was to provide a new objective for the old movement: the public look at everything that's going on and continue to push forward with deaf eyes; it is irritating to have to look where one is going at the same time as take in the entertainment. Many people have turned up in costume. Others in street clothes, others in evening dress. A kind of paralysis hangs over the people. What are they to do with themselves? Legs move, arms hang down or are crooked in other arms, eyes are overloaded, ears hear the orchestras which are out of reach, hair is untidy. The crowds have brought nothing with them in the first place, so what are they supposed to do with themselves?

Brintzinger, Beier-Müncheberg, Horn I and Horn II, always at the seam joining the two streams, push their way through to Entrance No. 4, a disturbance is reported there. The men from the Patrol & Security Service have already broken up the disturbance. But even this fracas fails to enliven the atmosphere. The management hits on the idea of removing the light fuses for one minute, simultaneously announcing over the loudspeaker: Eclipse for Lovers. This relaxes the tense atmosphere.

While the lights are out, an instant of panic, then better contact, which persists when the lights go on again.

The Bar Waitress

She has come down to the beer hall only for a minute. Her pouch: soft leather, hanging down from her waist. She pays from her pouch, in which, before paying, her fingers turn over the coins. She has a slice of meat loaf; when she has finished eating, she throws her serviette over the gravy left on her plate. Right after that she leaves. The glass with a tail-end of cola stands for quite a long time on the table like a miniature grave.

Tending the Carnival, 2

Horn I, Horn II, Häbel, Schleicher, Pichota and Putermann, under the command of Brintzinger, Karlota and Beier-Müncheberg, mingle in pairs with the public and get it into the mood. Karlota and his two men bring a dance band down from the stage, with them they form a line and wind their way like a kind of polonaise around the second floor, followed by the people. It is vital for the management to take ruthless advantage of any opportunity to improve the atmosphere: Beier-Müncheberg's commandos throw a young man out of the ballroom. That welds the people together. The public are gradually directed towards the focal points of the carnival (the beer hall downstairs, and the restaurant tables, wine only, upstairs). To everyone's surprise, buses arrive, bringing people from the Rhine-Main and Isar-Main areas; people already wearing funny hats and who on their way here, with the aid of some kind of cheap wine, have reached the stage of being able to pump new life into the carnival. There is a hitch at the entrance. The Security Service men try at first to exercise proper supervision; it is not long before their cordon is broken, people pour in and start singing and swaying. They storm the great staircases and those trying to come down are driven along in front of them to the beer hall on the third floor. Naturally, a great many gatecrashers have also managed to gain entrance in this way. But how are they to be tracked down? A few corners are roped off, and within them a strict inspection takes place. One or two persons are discovered who are unable to produce tickets.

Manfred Schmidt as Carnival Prince

Earlier in the evening, a delegation from the carnival committee had brought him the keys to the carnival building. He had been presented with the keys to the city several days before. Schmidt, still half-dressed, received the little delegation which handed him the keys to the building. They could have given him a better princess for the evening. He said so, and told them to pass it on to the carnival committee.

The Princess

Seven taxis were scarcely enough to accommodate the royal party. Many of the vehicles were overloaded—the committee economized where it shouldn't—slowing the column down to a crawl. MS had a car to himself. He had some more champagne. The princess got in beside him. She was not ugly, but wooden. Schmidt thought it would be difficult to make the public believe in her. He tried to start up a conversation and gave her some champagne. But he could not get anywhere with her, and she trembled when he put his arm around her, which was not altogether avoidable in the car.

Dispute with the Carnival Committee

Schmidt wasted precious time in a dispute with the carnival committee, who requested an interview with him as soon as he arrived. The committee was annoyed that Schmidt had publicly called them stingy. Schmidt found the discussion tiresome. He apologized, but this took time too, the committee being dissatisfied with the first draft of the apology. This led to a delay in the prince's entrance.

Stand by! 120 floodlights!

Midnight

Shouting from entrances Nos. 7 and 11, fanfares, new floodlights outside, all of a sudden: lights out. Everyone cheering in the momentary darkness, the orchestras descend from the stage carrying lighted candles, they march into the great ballroom at the top of the staircases. Five orchestras in there, each playing a different piece, enough to leave you gasping. Shouted orders. The General Manager appears.

Manfred Schmidt as Carnival Prince

It was past midnight by the time the procession of carnival prince, Manfred Schmidt, heralded by orchestras, mounted the staircase. The drum majorettes cleared a path, as best they could, for the triumphal procession. The prince, princess and retinue first paraded through the building. The first tableau was planned for the stage in the great ballroom (restaurant with wine only) which the musicians had vacated. For a moment, an observer might have thought—but of course this crowd had no observers—that one section of the column threading its way downstairs at the outer edge of the human wave pushing its way up would be so crushed against the railing that the railing would have to give way. In the event of disaster, the people would presumably have clung to one another and large sections of the human chain would have crashed to its death on the marble steps of the lower staircase. Had this happened, the carnival committee would have been found wanting. The row of 11 drum majorettes marched across the stage and formed a square in front of Manfred Schmidt and his court. The leading majorette drew her sword and strode right across the stage, holding the sword in front of her right thigh. She was then followed by the other majorettes. Before the 10 girls reached the edge of the stage, the column divided; now they marched in two parallel lines back to their point of departure. The leading majorette stood in the centre of the stage and saluted. This performance took place in the ballrooms (wine only), in the beer halls on the third floor and then on the first floor.

Death of the Bar Waitress

Due to the delay, the timing of the prince's entrance clashed with two raids which Police Commissioner Peiler organized shortly after midnight on the second and third floors. He did not expect to find anything. It was merely part of his method to walk through the principal rooms at least once with uniformed officers. Sometimes a person panics and gives himself away. Peiler walked across the bar, towards the counter, accompanied by the officers. When the waitress saw the police, she lost her nerve. It was later established that, at that moment, she swallowed poison; to the police officers, it looked as if she were hastily emptying a liqueur glass.

Peiler realized at once that something was wrong with her. They managed to remove her to hospital without attracting attention, but on arrival life was extinct, so no further steps were taken. A soft leather pouch was found in the bar. She had no permanent address; the reason for her sudden action could not be established. The festive spirit had gone out of the onlookers, despite the fact that the lifeless body had immediately been covered up and removed.

What Was Manfred Schmidt's Reaction?

News of the waitress' death reached Manfred Schmidt just as he was preparing to enter the great ballroom on the second floor at the head of his procession. After being informed of the death, he felt that any further processions would be out of place. The prince and his retinue later withdrew to the rooms in the cellar and were supplied with food and drink. MS had to decide whether to try his luck with one of the attractive ladies-in-waiting or call up his wife, Helena. He was too tired to start anything. He invested the remnant of his charm in the carnival princess, a Frau M., who was considered influential and might be of use to him one day. What good were the little teenage witches to him when he was that tired?

Outcome of the Carnival

After mature reflection—and in spite of his dispute with the carnival committee—Manfred Schmidt came to the conclusion that, all things considered, the carnival had been a success. Not a complete success, but no worse than no carnival at all. The committee was also satisfied with the outcome of the carnival.

II
The Person

In contrast to the nineteenth century, we are today in a position to predict to some extent the future development of industrial society. We are faced with the phenomenon that changing industrial society will probably demand the same qualities from all classes of society, and I would list these qualities as follows: first, reliability; second, mobility; third, a grasp of world issues. These three demands require explanation.

Hellmut Becker

Not to thrust one's hand into the jaws of fate, but, as soon as fate opens its jaws, to look around for a different fate.

Beethoven-Schmidt

Curriculum Vitae

Manfred Schmidt was born prematurely on 21 February 1926, in Thorn, West Prussia, son of GP Dr Manfred Schmidt and his wife Erika, née Scholz. He attended the local German primary school and later, high school. He left to volunteer for the air force in spring 1943. When the unit was to be incorporated into the Waffen-SS, he deserted, together with his friend K., and escaped to Switzerland. They took the route across Lake Constance, where his friend K. knew someone and had a concealed boat.

After his arrest in Switzerland, Schmidt appealed to a former acquaintance of his mother's for help. Aided by that kind friend, he and K. managed to escape from the internment camp to Zürich.

Immediately after the end of the tiresome war, Schmidt was employed by an oil company and sent to Sydney, Australia. He spent some happy years there until he was transferred back to a resuscitated Europe in 1951.

At the end of 1951, he took over an executive post with the firm of B. & Quamp Ltd.; soon afterward, the oil company in Australia, which he had just left, collapsed. Schmidt had no more influence on this bankruptcy than on Hitler's seizure of power in 1933 or the outbreak of war in 1939, but he saw it coming and got out in time. At B. & Quamp Ltd., he was popular both with his inferiors and the directors. His ability to adapt quickly to new situations distinguished him from his rivals. Since February, Schmidt has been married to Helena K., sister of his old friend K.

Memories of a Love Affair

I met F. in Sydney. In those days, I was still young and full of enthusiasm. She had some pull with the company and managed to get me a few days off, and we spent some unforgettable days together. She then flew back to Europe. From Alexandria, I received a telegram in which she asked my advice: a fly or something had stung her while swimming, and she asked whether or not she should have her leg amputated, as the doctors advised. She wanted me to make the decision for her. I later found out she had already been dangerously ill for some hours when she wired, but she was waiting for my reply. Naturally I wired back: amputate, fully concur with doctors. I had also consulted my own doctor. Years later, I met her again. Quite a young woman, six months younger than myself, perhaps. She could still go swimming in spite of her stump.

M. Sch. Acquires a Tan

He lay in the sun, and when his face had that degree of heat which, according to experience, turns to brown—a lengthy procedure, and very hard on the eyes: red-rimmed, because they could not stand the bright light—pimples developed on various parts of his face which ruined the whole thing. He said to himself: A person is only vulnerable as long as he has an objective. Verdun and Stalingrad are classic examples of how leaders run into difficulty because they have committed themselves to certain definite objectives. For example, you will never conquer a woman when you set out to do so.

Manfred Schmidt Meets Gitta, Who Later Becomes His Girlfriend

In July 1954, in response to a friend's appeal, Schmidt became involved in an unpleasant blackmail affair. Gitta P., at that time the mistress of one of his friends, received threatening letters from a former landlady. But she could not bring herself to part with the considerable sums of money demanded. Besides, there was no assurance that, once payment was made, the blackmailer would not make further demands. Schmidt solved the dilemma without payment being necessary. (He had the blackmail victim go to the police and file a report of attempted blackmail.) When this settled the matter, he was, of course, the hero of the day, and the woman swamped him with her friendship. For Schmidt, however, this led to trouble with his friend. Gitta P. was the type that leads to trouble. Schmidt was willing to help, but not be taken advantage of. Within a very short time, he became sick of this trouble. Gitta's girlfriend P. had driven a friend's car without a driver's licence and had an accident; she managed to get hold of Gitta, who did have a license and seated herself in the only slightly damaged vehicle. Interrogated by the police, she was forced to admit that, at the time of the accident, she had not been behind the wheel. In this hopeless situation, she again sought Schmidt's' assistance. But he could not stand these helpless creatures who make a permanent condition of their helplessness. The very proximity of such unfortunate people is noxious. It is best to become involved only with people who are consistently lucky. With women, that is not always possible; but to a certain extent, instinct tells one that it is impossible to love carriers of misfortune. Needless to say, Schmidt gave the girl the benefit of his advice. But that was as far as his interest went.

He Wins Over a Waitress

Are you just helping out, or do you work here permanently? The waitress said: Temporarily. He watched her intelligent movements as she cleared away the debris on the table. Temporarily helping out? No, permanently. But I don't know for how long. He disliked the previous employees, not because they did not bring him what he ordered but because of the unintelligent movements with which they served it. Nothing is more important than intelligent service, he said. She would bring him his coffee at the precise moment he placed the last morsel in his mouth. She could not help laughing at her own timing; soft creases at the sides of her neck when she laughed, but also when she did not.

He left her a handsome tip and continued to do so for the next few weeks; he exchanged remarks with her and tipped her. Thus Schmidt gradually won over the waitress.

He Fortifies Himself

Red wine, liverwurst and bread produced a layer of cement which completely lined his stomach. This enabled him to keep going.

He Observes a Waiter

On his buttocks, the waiter carries a pouch divided into two compartments. Acutely sensitive to every movement of this pouch. While he is standing around, he fingers the loose change inside it. In this restaurant, coffee is served by the pot only.

Manfred Schmidt Calls on His Former Girlfriend L. in Her Last Hours

One perfect sunny and blue-sky day—after breakfast, which he managed to have at seven, although most of the coffee shops do not open till later—Schmidt thought he would like to call on L. The air was still cool. He went to see L., with whom he had spent some pleasant days in Trident not long before; but now she was quite ill. Still, he hoped she would not make things too difficult for him.

L. opened the door wearing a silk kimono, white with a pattern of cherry blossoms, tied with a sash; she had pulled it around her in bed because she felt cold. A pretty face, much too small, around which her head had grown to normal adult size. Small hands, body, limbs of various age-categories. As soon as he entered, she had to answer the phone, and that gave him a chance to have a good look at her again and take her all in.

When she had finished phoning (in bed again now, a travelling alarm clock next to her pillow, everything else nice and tidy too), he tried to start something with her, but she turned away. Probably he had neglected her too long. He got off the edge of the bed and went into the next room to turn on the little radio and stirred the cup of coffee she had left there for him. Soon it occurred to him for the second time that day that he might be able to persuade her, after all. But because of her previous refusal, this notion evaporated. Before he had finished his coffee—and when he looked across again to the radio—the light had come on behind the panel.

He made himself comfortable. When the doctor arrived, she asked him to go into another room. When the doctor left, he wanted to give her a cold shower, an old-fashioned remedy said to be good for stomach-aches, but she didn't want that either. He sat listening to the radio and told her to call if she wanted him. After a time, he went over to her again and asked if she liked him at all, if it made any difference to her whether he stayed or not. He reminded her of the time in Trident. She groaned, lying on her side, the quilt drawn up to almost cover her head, or at least the thin, sheet-covered edge, the way one stuffs a handkerchief in one's mouth and bites down on it. He tried to massage her stomach, but she pushed him away when he went too far. He criticized her for her attitude and her coldness.

As the afternoon wore on, her condition grew worse. She had cramps, but he was still too offended to pay any attention. He did not go near her. It was only when she had been groaning for rather a long time that he phoned the doctor. He did his best to distract her by trying to get her in the mood. But she was grouchy, and whatever he did hurt her.

It was difficult to get hold of her doctor. At first, because of the way she had insulted him, Schmidt had not made any serious effort. He tried to cheer her up, she was getting steadily worse, and to kiss her; she didn't understand, she didn't know what he wanted, behaved awkwardly when he put his lips on hers. Not until much later did he realize that he was in the presence of someone who was, in fact, dying.

He was scared, but then he felt he ought to give her one more thrill before she died. In fact, he made preparations, but they bogged down in the clash of emotions. He remade the bed for her and carried her around the room. She whimpered incessantly, and remained doubled up while he unfolded and shook out a clean sheet. Then he laid her on the freshly made bed; phoned various doctors, even called a hospital, but none of them wanted to send anybody. She died at the very moment he seemed to be getting somewhere. By being sufficiently insistent on the phone, he finally achieved success. Fifteen minutes later, the doctor was there.

Manfred Schmidt in an Embarrassing Situation

Schmidt was embarrassed by the large bluish-brown bruise on his neck given him by Aina Sp. His shirt was rather crumpled, and there were probably some red marks on his collar, he'd had no time to go home that morning. He had to go to the meeting, at which directors would be present, the way he was. In that state, he took in nothing of what was being said. The bruise was almost exactly below his jaw and practically impossible to hide. That day, one of the directors asked him for a brief resume. Schmidt was obliged to ask for leave to remain seated during his short address. That evening, due to lack of consideration, Schmidt was saddled with entertaining some company guests from Venezuela. He was afraid they would be able to smell where he had been, especially in view of the greenish-blue bruise which he inspected at regular intervals in a cloakroom mirror. But it is possible to survive even such an evening as this. Though it was all most unpleasant, sitting around in that shirt and being asked questions. What was he to do? Quit that life because it led to such unpleasant evenings?

Christmas Eve

Schmidt had sacrificed everything that he did not want, but he still had nothing. He proceeded on the principle that every sacrifice cleared the way for something else and was thus indirectly profitable; and if one can get rid of enough things one does not want, one is bound gradually to get close to the things one does want. All that happened, however, was that the sacrifices impoverished him—which did not alter the fact that he had no desire to be without the sacrifices either. In former years, it had been his practice to celebrate Christmas Eve with some of the men from the office; now he has given up that too.

He follows the slow dying of the city that is to be observed only on Christmas Eve, since the city's resemblance to a corpse on ordinary Sundays and holidays, when one wakes up and looks out onto the street, is a *fait accompli*. But on Christmas Eve one can watch the streets slowly dying. It would be dangerous to fall ill now, for it would be impossible to find a doctor. He is looking for a restaurant where he can get something to eat. He asks some people; they direct him to a place they believe is still open. But when he arrives it is closed. Search for shelter alternating with human kindness, neither of which, however, is capable of locating a restaurant for him. When he does find a place open, he asks the waiter, who politely puts an arm around his shoulder (human kindness), whether there is any room. But every seat is taken, and he has to wander several times among the occupied tables (search for shelter). A customer asks him: Are you sure you don't bite? For a moment it looks as if there might be room, if they squeezed up a bit, but his hopes are dashed. Although the waiter sticks by him to the very end and gives him advice, he is obliged to leave this ark in the dead city. The morning papers had already given up printing political news. People are engrossed in their holiday preparations and handle the day with great care so that nothing will happen to impair the mood. After a while, Schmidt finds a restaurant where he can get some coffee. But here too he has to leave right after. Two women emerge from the night club one floor up, with their escorts who are putting on their coats. The women are still warm: they go over to the jukebox and warm themselves before it as if it were a little stove. Just one more please, they say, when the proprietor tries to prevent them from feeding the machine. They order a taxi and leave it waiting outside until the music is finished.

Schmidt follows the slow death of the city; he celebrates Christmas Eve by getting an impression of the dead city. He calls up girlfriends, though he doesn't expect them to be home. He feels a great longing for them and cannot remember why he left them. He calls up A. and is nonplussed when he hears her voice.

She is alone, and he invites her over. He sends a taxi to pick her up. When she rings twice and is at the door: a miracle is born to us this day. Schmidt brings out a bottle of champagne and rests his head on her shoulder. He shows her how much her nearness means to him; he explains at length how much he has changed; yes, he even believes he loves her now. But he does not grasp the situation, and respects her request not to fall on her immediately. He does not want to become involved. She stays over, but things are no longer the same. His nervous system has been overtaxed by the excitement of her coming, and although he is no longer scared of the dead holidays after Christmas Eve, since he knows he has company now, he needs a breather. He cannot get rid of the tension in his stomach area. He finds it impossible to approach her successfully, and talks rather too much about this point. He loses the child—if one may compare his altered emotions since she came to him with a child or a miracle—and his subsequent success comes too late to do any good. It is in a way something like a second miracle, this success, but Schmidt has meanwhile reverted to his pattern. His victory helps convince him. Everything is as before (the gamble before knowing a city, the gamble before knowing a woman).

She visited him once more between Christmas and New Year. Then life began again. Right after New Year's Eve there was a lot going on. He lost sight of her.

Application

My name is Manfred Schmidt. I am married, no children, and was born 21 February 1926, in Thorn, West Prussia, the legitimate offspring of Dr Manfred Schmidt, general practitioner, and his wife Erika, née Scholz. I attended the local primary school and later went to secondary school, from which I graduated (wartime matriculation) in the spring of 1942. In the summer of 1945, after a brief period in the army and some time in Switzerland, I accepted a post as engineer with the firm of Pignatelli & Cie. in Sydney, Australia. Immediately after my appointment as vice manager, I gave up the position, interesting though it was, and applied to the firm of B. & Quamp Ltd. in Frankfurt-am-Main. I worked for this company for a number of years in various places. Since I was anxious not to devote my entire career to one type of business, I decided in March of last year to join the firm of Helldorf & Co., lumber wholesalers, a company offering me excellent opportunities to gain experience in the import of teakwoods and where I was also put in charge of sales. I have no reason to be dissatisfied with the broad scope of my duties with this firm. Nevertheless, I am prompted to submit the enclosed application in the belief that it is likely to improve my prospects.

III
Specimen Love Story
(The Time with Gitta)

Gitta as the Young Mistress of an Old Farmer

She is embarrassed by her partner's teeth and therefore keeps her mouth closed. She sticks her tongue into a bottle of Coca-Cola but can't get into the narrow opening and has to laugh terribly. Her tongue vanishes into her mouth. Her arms, very pale, with vaccination marks, muscular under the white skin, blueish where the veins are; like a dog, she pokes her head towards the carnival farmer to tell him something; voice, rather high. With a wide gap between her front teeth, which makes her mouth seem attractive; she keeps her lips narrow so no one can see the gap.

She yawns, her mouth narrow, she wants to tell this man something but is stopped short by the unpleasant front teeth he displays and cannot bring herself to laugh again for a long time. Her golden-brown eyes, with some reflections in them, looking quietly around, beyond, till once again she pokes her head forward like a dog and says something in a high voice.

She was ashamed to be seen by Schmidt in the company of this farmer dressed as a pierrot. The man was trying to paw her while he swallowed small mouthfuls of wine. Needless to say, Schmidt rescued the girl at once from this impossible situation. He took her home. That first night with Gitta was a complete failure. She became impertinent. While making an effort to be nice and gloss over his fiasco, she became impertinent.

The Trip to the Isle of Sylt

It rained the whole day. Once, quite early in the morning, they ran through the rain down to the beach in their bathing suits. Dull grey sea, luminous white crests on the breakers. They just splashed about a bit at the edge of the water but did not dare go in because of the wind. Oddly enough, there was no warning notice for bathers.

The rest of the day they spent in bed reading, each surrounded by books and magazines. Now and again one of them would read something out to the other. At other times, Schmidt would have a long sleep while Gitta read her novels. He was not interested in reading. Nevertheless, he found this rainy day pleasanter than those previous exhausting days of sunshine when one always had the feeling of missing something.

At a Party of Some Importance, to Which He Takes His Attractive Girlfriend Gitta

Everyone was aware that Schmidt knew something about Emperor Frederick II in Sicily (from some excursion or other he had made to Sicily). In order to impress the directors, who had also come to the party, he brought up this very subject. It was most embarrassing for Gitta. But she didn't want to interrupt him because she could not be sure how he would react.

With his intense blue eyes and the hard black stars in them. He had a handsome head and it probably functioned quite efficiently, but it was put to very limited use. He had some kind of inhibition about using it. She brought him some cigarettes and a glass of the champagne with which the waiters were standing around. She tried to pry him loose from the group in which he was holding forth.

A Bone of Contention Between Gitta and MS

I can't stand it when he says:

Let's not jump the gun.

Tomorrow is another day.

How do we know we'll still be here tomorrow?

Let's wait and see what happens.

That's a long way off yet.

There's no telling what will happen between now and then.

Some built-in inhibition prevents him from using his intelligence, unless he is dealing with things he can see. His intelligence is the slave of those eyes.

Memories of a Love Affair

I hate Sundays because they show how little is left when there's no work to do. On a Sunday during the war, I had to fill in for the supervisor at our Air Force hospital. The doctor in charge and most of the nurses were away. About eleven o'clock, a Frenchman was brought in who had been shot by mistake. He was one of the foreign workers. The idea was to try and repair the unintentional damage at the hospital without having to report the case. Our instructions were to keep the workman on a stretcher till the doctor came back. He lay there fairly quietly, now and again complaining, but we could never make out what he was saying. He had hollow cheeks and coarse lips, the tips of which protruded like a child's. Occasionally, someone would walk by outside on the street. The hospital was housed in what used to be a school. Those empty streets made me feel physically uncomfortable. The Frenchman died bit by bit in the course of the afternoon, but not quite, so that, in the midst of the food and cups of coffee with which we had surrounded him, in case he felt like having something, he went on quietly moaning. He had ugly hair, plastered down with water, which had survived the shooting in that plastered-down condition. He would not let us touch the wound. In the afternoon, I phoned E., who had a wartime job in a hotel in this small town, and asked her to come over.

We fixed ourselves up in a secluded corner of the primary school now serving as a hospital; it was the first time we had improvised anything like that (which corresponds after all to the quite natural instincts of childhood and nest building), and although I didn't count on success that day, as I felt I was too ill-at-ease to satisfy her, she said something very nice about it to me on a later occasion, and when we talk about it we still sometimes mention that Frenchman whom the doctor visited in the evening.

Reconciliation

A crisis between Schmidt and Gitta lasted nearly six months, without either of them becoming truly aggressive. Neither of them lost their temper, and it was almost all over when Gitta had a bright idea and they decided to take a trip. She would have had a lot more bright ideas if instead of a single happy afternoon it had been a whole series of them. But the exception was enough to give her the idea.

An impulsive stopover in the mountains, because they found the mountains impressive and wanted to make some decisions. So they got out and looked for a hotel. They could not get a room, but one of the big hotels still had a vacant bathroom. They took the bathroom, and the hotel fixed it up for them as best it could.

They ordered the full dinner, there was no choice, but they were compensated for the appreciable financial outlay by coming across an empty English biscuit tin when they were changing in their bathroom, and, pleased with their find, they appropriated it. Compared to their situation in the train, they felt much better off, and finally made up while they were waiting for the second course.

Later, they experimented to see if they fitted into the bathtub, which took up most of the space. But it was too narrow in there for two, and so they chose the operating table which had been brought in for them and set it up as a bed. It was a spotlessly clean room, the fresh white bed linen smelled of detergent, it was very hot, so hot their ears got red, they cleared away some black garments that lay around. Everything was so clean and tiled and so overheated, only artificial light in this little bathroom, pleasantly full from the large meal, now and again someone would hurry along the corridor outside, it was so hot they couldn't be careful too. They could think of no better way of showing they had made up than this. They could have devoured each other, but they confined themselves to being careless.

Gitta's Monologue

Should Gitta become a mother? Should she take steps? Act on her own, or ask Manfred Schmidt? Latest possible time is the end of the third month. During these days of doubt, Schmidt sent Gitta three red roses, delivered by a Fleurop messenger.

Manfred Schmidt Strays During This Period

The girl Carmela Pichota, alias Lastics, was born in 1926. At the age of 16 months, she fell into her mother's laundry tub, was lightly scalded, skin grafts, the child made a good recovery. No further incident until she was 17. As an army nurse, age 17, a love affair with a considerably older married man who was convalescing. As soon as he left the hospital, the affair was over for him. For her, that was a shock. Four abortions in one year, she was now 18. During the next couple of years, she studied home economics.

I ought never to have got involved with her. As a matter of fact, I disliked her. I had not noticed what an unlucky person she is.

His Girlfriend Gitta Is Not Going to Be a Mother Just Yet

This time she came to the restaurant quite changed and said something under her breath to one of the women sitting there. Whispered conversation. Her complexion was different, light-pale-flushed: white, olive. She lit a cigarette.

Can Love Be Aborted Too?

He carried his full tank of emotions to her in that unfamiliar city. Gitta had been waiting at the hotel since getting news from him. She had spent the morning shopping. He came these days from tough, smoke-filled morning conferences. The moment he was with her in the hotel, he drew a line under the stale, unprofitable mornings and abandoned himself to her. He did this so often, hammering away at the one point at which new emotions were showing, that soon there was nothing left of them.

(When he arrived, he was bubbling over with affection, and completely wrapped her up in it. He radiated almost the whole afternoon. Still fresh from the frustrating activities of the morning. Her mind was a freshly raked garden, and not only her mind, arms too, legs willing and surrendering to him. Lips, warm and soft. Then he stopped radiating.)

Separation

Schmidt and Gitta withdrew for a week to Krefeld, where they didn't know a soul, in order to give birth to their separation in peace. Gitta attended to that for both of them. She was exhausted when the outcome of the seclusion on which she had pinned her hopes was separation. Schmidt financed a trip for her to the North Sea and went with her for a few days: he let Gitta sunbathe in Rantum. He was satisfied with this solution and only half-believed in the separation, as he was with Gitta every day, he enjoyed freedom in theory and attachment in practice. He looked forward to a winter with Gitta, for he assumed that their relationship would now blossom again. Greatly to his surprise, however, once he had left Rantum, the separation turned out to be a *fait accompli*. You become entangled with guilt. But what else can you do?

He Is Suddenly Reminded of Gitta

A streak of hair below the kneecap growing from right to left. Otherwise there was no resemblance. The woman was sitting with her legs crossed and wondered, although she did not raise her eyes from her newspaper, why the man—they were the only passengers in that compartment—was looking so fixedly at her knees.

Portrait of A Happy Girl with a Cold (G.)

She was chilled to the marrow, so she talked more than usual. Aspirin was no use at all. She had borrowed a man's pullover, which had to be brought specially from the cloakroom, and was wearing a fur jacket on top of that, but she was still cold. In front of her stood several hot toddies which the men at her table had ordered for her. Each of them wanted to buy her a drink, and the orders came before the men could agree on only one ordering or a few taking turns. She sat there bundled up as if in the depths of winter.

SERGEANT MAJOR HANS PEICKERT

I

The messenger in the service of the last Reich Chancellor but one before Hitler, from 1928 to 1933, was called Hans Peickert. In later years, he advanced to sergeant major. His parents and ancestors had been hardly more than serfs on some landed estates in West Prussia. At the age of 20, Peickert went to Berlin and entered the service of the said Herr von P. The cornucopia of rich gifts offered by politics and the new era was spilling its contents over the Conservatives, who had stood fast in troubled times. As a messenger, Peickert became part of his master's intricate communications network. The new opulence coming after the age-old Prussian shabbiness, although it only benefited his master, convinced Peickert of the dawning of a new era.

The Nationalist Right's Methods of Government

After the downfall of the monarchy, the nationalist right looked on the Germany that remained as a kind of large fief to be divided up. Friends and respected enemies joined together to form a powerful right wing. In the Baltic provinces, in Berlin, in rebellious Saxony, in Bavaria, this right wing quickly made the obdurate see reason. With animal persistence, the right wing built a facade of duty. Under this guise of duty, it set out to trap men.

Peickert Trapped Since Birth

West Prussia had offered no opportunity for Peickert. In von P.'s service there was no opportunity for him either. Peickert's status excluded him from sharing in the political spoils. Since working for his master required all Peickert's energies, it was immaterial whether he worked for this one master or for many in West Prussia. The only thing he had control over was his girlfriend Magda S. In 1932, he attempted to make her work for him on the streets. As a result, he was reported to the police. Von P. warned him. Soon after, von P. joined Hitler's cabinet. There were signs that his downfall was imminent. Peickert thought this was the moment to get away from his master. He asked to be allowed to join the army.

The Statesman Refused to Recognize His Imminent Downfall

Von P., who had just been appointed Hitler's Vice Chancellor, ordered Peickert to remain. Time and again von P. tried in his speeches and conversations to salvage something for himself and his friends. After losing his post as Vice Chancellor in 1934, he tried at least to retain his substitute post as German ambassador in Vienna. The annexation of Austria did away with that. One of von P.' s closest collaborators was shot. At the end of 1934, Peickert was accepted as a recruit in the German army.

II

After leaving von P.' s service, Peickert was filled with new hope. The elimination of the old masters now seemed to Peickert to betoken the extension of the cornucopia to all the faithful. In the army, he had advanced in 1935 from recruit to private; in 1936, from private to private, first class; in 1938, from private, first class, to corporal. With the expansion of the army immediately before the outbreak of war, he made the leap to sergeant. During the first year of the war, he became a sergeant major. This gradual rise from someone who is of no importance with very little pay, to someone who is of slightly more importance with a little more pay, did not correspond to Peickert's idea of increasing the scope of his opportunities. He now put his hopes in the war. The war was supposed to expand the *Lebensraum* of the German people. Peickert pictured this as having a wide application.

War Conducted According to Prison Regulations

In Peickert's life so far, there had been nothing but disappointment. The urge to imitate his parents, to obey the lord of the manor, had betrayed him; no one gave him credit for this good intention or any derivative of it. The urge to be popular in school did him no good. His hopes in his great master in Berlin deceived him, since his master merely exploited him. But his hopes in the National Socialists deceived him too, for his gradual advancement in the army, the weapons and equipment, the promise of improved accommodation after the war, the prospect of a chance to increase his knowledge at a military school, offered no prospect of the radical change Peickert was seeking. Finally, the war itself was a bitter disappointment. The troops marching into Poland were disciplined. Soldiers found looting were frequently shot. The shooting of this or that enemy or of impertinent civilians brought no change in the overall situation. In France, things were much the same.

Pearls of Wisdom, Store of Childhood Memories

Use your head where it does the most good.
Keep under cover and sit it out.
Click goes the brain, yackety yack goes the billygoat.
First you're cheated, then you lie, you've smartened up.
Let the kike have it in the schnoz.
Don't ask why, say that's why.
Go fly a kite.
That's that.

Memory: Big holiday when the county council gave official permission for the storming of the pharmacy in S., which had been proved to be handling contaminated drugs. Pots of ointment smashed against the walls. Fire broke out later on in the so-called laboratory.

Childhood memories of the pregnant housekeeper at the manor: the local doctor had attempted to turn the child around in the woman's belly as it was lying incorrectly. Injuries had resulted. All Christmas, the woman lay bleeding to death on a stretcher in the laundry room (the birth was supposed to be kept a secret). The bleeding exhausted the woman more and more. Yawning. Fear, as the blood ran out.

Lullaby:

Trickle, trickle, dribble drip.
A nasty gash, beyond a doubt
Dolly's gone and hurt herself,
All the sawdust's running out.

Peickert's Appearance

Deep chest, short neck: well suited for a resonant voice. The lower part of his body solidly built. Face with no special features: nervous areas around the temples, dun-coloured hair; hard, calloused lips, or rather: shutting apparatus. No fixed habits: like many emigrants from what used to be Central Europe (unlike farmers or peasants), not settled-hard to get hold of, a shell with many uses but housing a strong desire for expansion. This figure was encased in the smart uniform of a sergeant major with a lanyard. His cap was pinched right and left at the front and was too small for his head; he wore it at a slight angle. Raucous bark on duty, modulated transmitter in private, i.e. in business.

Special Type of Intelligence

He was obsessed with the idea of rousing the movement 'yes' in Lieutenant Tacke's face (sensation; sign; flaring up of the old promise: good). Peickert's language, his whole body in fact, was attuned to that particular form of transmission which would prompt Tacke's reaction. Without consideration for truthful utterance, consequences or harm, Peickert extracted material from his environment, re-minted it, re-forged it and poured it into this one purpose: to summon understanding in Tacke's face. Bankrupt, entangled in untenable utterances and promises, in a state of inner turmoil, Peickert took leave of his superior.

Business Training

At school, Peickert bartered stolen food for true confession and adventure stories. He bartered his talents for Herr von P.' s favour, which was of no use to him. He bartered his girlfriend so the charge of procuring would be dropped. He bartered his life expectancy, in a certain sense his very life, for the opportunity of advancement in the army. If Peickert had children, they might have achieved the leap to still-greater barter status, the leap to an academic career, for example. They could never have become members of the upper class. Peickert did not want to have children with an academic career; as things stood now, he did not want any children just yet, he wanted to live himself.

Duty and Life

Peickert spent the summer of 1940 in France. His division was resting in Lille, France. In Metz, Peickert met Angélique Danatier, who later became his fiancée. As soon as he could exert sufficient power over her, he offered her services to officers at the garrisons of Lille, Metz, Montmédie and Rheims. He also trafficked in weapons, English cigarettes and leave passes, as well as a variety of commissariat goods. On duty, Peickert was the perfect image of a German sergeant major.

III

The garrison town of Lille in France lies in a valley. Behind the railway district lie the barracks, already used to quarter German troops during the First World War. Some private houses had also been requisitioned for billeting purposes. One of these houses, Villa Hébert, situated on the road leading out of the city towards the southeast, had been allocated to Sergeant Major Peickert and his staff. In the house on the right lived the French mayor appointed by the occupying forces, on the left lived counterintelligence men. Peickert's duties in Lille consisted of being in charge of a training unit, supervising a number of local factories and conducting some of the Lille headquarters' correspondence. Moreover, as a favour, Peickert had taken over the temporary running of an anti-aircraft battery nearby that was without a quartermaster. Except for the times when he was away on duty, the day began for Peickert at 6 a.m. with a company inspection. Followed by the hoisting of the flag. Shortly before 7, Peickert appeared at the office of the anti aircraft battery where he took care of some of the correspondence. At 9 a.m. every fourth day, Peickert reported to the commandant, every sixth day to the Lille counterintelligence headquarters (next door), as well as to the army and air-force units where he had friends. From 11 to 2, he inspected the work of the training unit and had lunch. From 3 to 6, he attended to correspondence. At 6, Peickert usually went off duty.

The performance of his duties allowed for numerous variations. For example, by doing some of his work ahead of time, the hours allotted to correspondence between 7 and 9 in the morning and 3 and 6 in the afternoon could be saved. For the flag hoisting and company inspection, a sergeant was sufficient every second and third day. Inspection of the training unit's work could be spun out. Peickert had the reputation of deserving support. If he had been away from his unit for a week, no one would have noticed; in 1940 and 41, Peickert made no trip that took him away for more than two and a half days. He had 620 men and 12 noncoms under him. In Villa Hébert, his immediate subordinates were Sergeants Freyer and Müller-Segeberg.

Business Report for 1940, upto the Crisis of Winter 1941/42

From July 1940, Peickert's business projects, as they existed at a level below the strict performance of his duties, were as follows:

October

Sale of weapons	4,000
English cigarettes	300
Payments from Angélique and Marika	800
Profit on one lot nylons to Halberstadt, Oschersleben and Wernigerode; 10% commission	1,200
Commissariat goods, profit	600
Miscellaneous	30
Plus pay (cash)	138
Total	**RM 7,338**

July

Payments from Angélique	120
Plus pay (cash)	138
Total	**RM 258**

August/September

Payments from Angélique	300
Payments from Marika G., from mid-Sept.	280
Profit on commissariat goods, food & drink	100
Plus pay (cash)	276
Manoeuvre allowance	32
Total	**RM 988**

The year from November 1940 to November 1941 could be called his first fiscal year. November 1940 saw the establishment of business connections with Army Command Areas IV and VI. The November successes were followed by a trip to former Poland with the aim of buying some property near Posen. In January, he bought a property in Graudenz, and established his residence in that town. Peickert's peripheral activities now included: commission on Angelique's and Marika's earnings; trading in lumber, gasoline, small arms, tobacco and commissariat goods. That year brought in 43,000 marks cash, a property worth 17,000 marks, as well as a number of prospects for the future. Peickert sensed the approaching crisis of the winter of 1941. From November 1941 until February 1942, he did no business, since he was afraid of large-scale controls and inspection of supplies behind the lines sparked by the winter's disasters on the eastern front. He waited, so to speak, until the extent of the danger became clear.

Motto: A Joy to Live

A well-known rightwing author said: It is a joy to live! On the other hand, the song says: Who joy desires, who joy selects, his earthly lot will e'er be pain; who ne'er desires nor chooses joy, his earthly lot will ne'er be pain. Peickert hoped his lot would 'ne'er be pain'.

That was why he did not make a beeline for joy. It gave him quite a sense of satisfaction to play hamster that winter of 1941–42, i.e. to have sufficient reserves on hand to guard against any contingency. But there was also some joy, as a byproduct. Unforgettable, the twilight mood of the first air raids on Berlin, spent in the zoo air-raid shelter. Unforgettable, too, the quick trip on 31 December 1941 to Wannsee. Predated files passed on to superiors on the preceding day seemed to leave no doubt that Peickert was carrying out his duties in Lille.

Achievements of the Reich Railways

Until well into the summer of 1942, the train schedules throughout western Germany as well as in France remained reasonably reliable. Delays were announced with up to 36 hours' notice and could be ascertained by telephone at a distance of 400 to 600 miles. Now and again, the airport administration would offer Peickert a seat in a fighter plane that happened to be making a quick trip. The Balkans, which became very important to Peickert in 1942, could only be reached by plane. On one occasion, Peickert bartered a trainload of gasoline that was on its way from a Stettin refinery to Kielce and was threatened with inspection and line disruption for a much smaller troop transport on a private siding in Central Germany.

Sense of Fear

Peickert carried two wallets, with amounts ranging from 600 to 1,000 marks, whether he was travelling or not. When his reserves dropped below 600, he felt afraid. A sense of insecurity paralysed him, made him incapable as well as suspicious of decisions, since he was afraid of panic causing the wrong decisions. His suspicions also increased his sense of fear. Hence the constant provision for the future in the form of numerous wallets, some of which were carefully concealed. Stalingrad, the annihilation of the Sixth Army before Christmas 1942 and the dark days of January 1943 threw a shadow over everything. It also gave Peickert's affairs a kind of consecration, an atmosphere of imminent danger, which Peickert found agreeable because it reflected the proportion of his state of fear better than the holidays, his time at the beach, any special announcements, a promotion or preparations for Christmas would have done.

IV

In 1943, Peickert's travels extended to Romania, to the Peloponnese, to Italy, Denmark, various places in Germany, the General Government (formerly Poland), in one case even to the Eastern Territories and the Memel. He spent Christmas in the Tyrol. In Italy, he got hold of a large quantity of textiles. In Greece, he made no purchases, since what was offered was confiscated merchandise; he was afraid that goods which had once been taken away might bring bad luck. Since the spring of 1943, his main source had been trading in gasoline and the Lille–Romania link for all types of merchandise.

A Good Man: Army Judge Döhmer

Peickert was suspicious of a friend who was under no obligation to him: Döhmer, army judge of the Sixth Army in the Crimea, later in Romania. Since Peickert could see no motive for this friendship, he suspected a trap. Kindness was something Döhmer applied to everyone within reach. Like many men trained to associate with vanishing power, Döhmer had the patience to gather men into his net through kindness, on the assumption that they would be of use to him once he had hold of them. So this kindness was really nothing but rapaciousness in another form. Peickert was afraid of Döhmer's kindness. On the other hand, he did not want to offend the powerful man. So they were friends.

Fleeting Contact with Arlette

After her first visit (two days after they met at Cafe Vaterland) to Peickert's apartment in Berlin, Sächsische Strasse 68, she very soon came again and even laid in a small supply of contraceptives. She put them behind some books in the living room, within arm's reach. Peickert never came again to that apartment in the Sächsische Strasse. All plans for meeting Arlette collapsed.

Check Zone

Military police were massed in a north–south zone between Fürstenwalde and Schwiebus. Since the fall of 1943, Peickert had preferred to travel close to the front rather than through Germany, barter prospects also becoming more promising closer to the front, i.e. towards the east and southeast.

List of Assets

February 1944: 1,000 gallons of sunflower oil in the Olteanu warehouse in Bucharest; a contingent of farm workers on various estates in Podolia; a brothel in Lille with connections to Posen and Kamenez-Podolsk; cash and papers for after the war; valuables in Mannheim, Berlin, Koblenz; two vineyards in the South of France, acquired in exchange for a chance for three French prisoners-of-war (factory managers) to escape; some 45,000 gallons of fuel scattered through various depots in northern Romania, the Carpathians, Czechoslovakia; a boxcar of lumber en route from the Carpathians to southern Germany; three Romanian associates; six bales of textiles from Italy; a garden plot in Blankenese, near Hamburg; properties in Posen and Graudenz; supply of 80 travel-warrant blanks; stocks of cigarettes, food concentrates, leather goods; a partnership in a Leipzig fur business; a concealed Opel car; complete combat equipment for eight men (including machine pistols and snowshirts).

V

In February 1944, an officer in Lille brought charges against Peickert for procuring. At the time, Peickert was spending his first home leave in the headquarters area of Panzer General Famula, near Targulfrumos, Romania.

Barter and Absolute Values

Greater Germany—i.e. the old Reich, occupied and allied territories—is full of opportunities for barter. Hence there is always a way out somewhere, a concealed point for saving one's life. Like minefields scattered about: absolute values. Values such as: a German soldier is not a procurer, spell death to the transgressor. At this point, barter possibilities cease.

Threat

On 12 February 1944, 24 Russian tank brigades together with some 30 rifle divisions attacked the Targulfrumos sector of the German front. General Famula's tanks were immobilized due to lack of petrol.

Relationship to Panzer General Famula

Peickert had never spoken to the general. Admiration for the Panzer leader had spread through the staffs of the Sixth and Eighth Armies like a contagion. The general, well known even in peacetime for his bold exploits at horse shows, was in command of the best tanks the German Army ever had. His general disbelief in a non-victory, supported by the excellent equipment of his troops, rubbed off on his inferiors. At Targulfrumos, his division needed at least 60,000 gallons of petrol.

Peickert's Petrol Stocks within Reach of the Famula Army

About 3,000 gallons south-east of Jesny, 1,500 gallons west of Ileoai; train with 30,000 gallons in the Carpathians. These quantities could be obtained in a day and a half. A further 15,000 gallons could be brought up within two days. These basic stocks could be augmented by a further 10,000 gallons that Peickert was confident he could organize.

Can Peickert Afford to Act Spontaneously?

At first Peickert saw no danger in offering petrol to Famula. He still did not see his favourite general (whom he thought of as a cross between Tacke and the famous West Prussian equestrian Herr von Westrum) even when he went to inform him that he could supply the necessary quantities of petrol. The message was taken by an adjutant. The Famula tanks later destroyed a hundred Soviet tanks. As a result, the front could be advanced again as far as Jüpan sector.

Famula's Maxims

> Misgivings always arise. In defiance of them, the only people who achieve success are those capable of deciding to take a leap in the dark. For the future will show greater clemency in judging those who act than those who fail to act.
>
> *Famula*

> Once the terrain and the position have been inspected, the bold decision is usually the best one.
>
> *Famula*

The experienced supply officer multiplies normal consumption by three.

Famula

Capture

The day after the Panzer victory of Targulfrumos, the second-in-command, Colonel von Posselt, applied for a Knight's Cross for Peickert with the approval of General Famula. Peickert would have preferred a German Cross in gold. A German Cross in gold could have been awarded by any corps commander.

The application for the award of a Knight's Cross to Peickert was received at military personnel headquarters, and led to the arrest of Peickert who had been charged with living on the avails of prostitution. Peickert was removed to the military prison at Graudenz.

Escape on Parole?

Had it been possible to get out of the fortress prison of Graudenz for one day (on parole, for example), Peickert would have been able to reach the Kovno area or the Carpathians. He knew of a partisan hideout there.

General Famula Intervenes

The general said to his adjutant: We'll get Peickert out. To Dr Burdach, a National Socialist official at the headquarters, the general said: Peickert lent us a hand, we'll lend Peickert a hand. A lieutenant-colonel who was going to Berlin was instructed to do his utmost for Peickert. The lieutenant-colonel managed to get through by telephone from the Reich capital to the military prison at Graudenz. A few days later, a Major von F. was passing through

Graudenz. A member of the Sixth Army's quartermaster's staff, he brought greetings for Peickert. The message was received at the civilian prison in North Graudenz. It was transmitted to the military prison in the fortified zone, but the transmission was delayed, so the message did not arrive until after sentence had been carried out, i.e. after January 16th.

General von Posselt, successor to Famula (who was transferred to Poland), dictated the following letter, dated 24 November 1944, to the Military Court of Inquiry Prison at Graudenz:

> Re: Military prisoner Hans Peickert
>
> Subject: Official request
>
> Ref.: Sentence passed 3 August 1944
>
> I request support for the petition for reprieve on the part of the above-named. During the events at the front over the past year, Peickert has shown endurance, calm, an intelligent grasp, an ability to make decisions and, in particular, personal bravery, and a pardon therefore seems to me worthy of consideration. In view of the extreme shortage of personnel, Peickert is required here.
>
> Date:
>
> Signed:
>
> (General)

Help from von P.?

In response to a postcard he received at the end of 1944 from the Graudenz military prison, von P. sent a telegram via the Foreign Office to the Supreme Command, to be forwarded to the military zone commander in Danzig: REQUIRE SERGEANT MAJOR PEICKERT AS DRIVER IN ANKARA. VON P.

Last Meal

Peickert wanted nothing to eat.

Sentence Carried Out

On the eve of 16 January, Peickert was still confident he would be able to escape. The prison chaplain inquired as to his last wish. Peickert asked for a novel. (Until then, he had hardly ever found time to read.) The next morning, while Russian assault troops were approaching Graudenz, Peickert was shot in the yard of the Graudenz fortress by a firing squad. Before he was executed, the reasons for the sentence were read out to him.

VI

Posthumous career: *Infantryman's Bulletin,* Issue No. 234, appeared in July 1962: 'Hans Peickert, Holder of the Knight's Cross'.

Hans F. writes in the Preface:

> Whenever the fortunes of war threatened to desert the simple man, events at the front saw the emergence of the action of an individual whose personality turned the tide. And so it was at Targulfrumos. A whole Panzer division, under the command of General Famula, lay immobilized through lack of fuel. When, all of a sudden, supplies came rolling in! Hans Peickert, holder of the Knight's Cross, fallen at the front, had obtained the necessary quantities of petrol from depots behind the lines. The result was a fantastic victory. The front could be advanced as far as the Jüpan sector! May this issue of the *Bulletin* display the spirit that Hans Peickert, holder of the Knight's Cross, has bequeathed to us as a priceless legacy!

> I particularly wish to take this additional opportunity of paying homage to our fallen comrades.
>
> Hans F.

42,000 copies of the pamphlet were printed, of which 41,600 were sold. Further use of the dead Peickert could easily be made with a reissue of the pamphlet after expiry of the eight-month copyright period.

A CHANGE OF CAREER

I

We who are new, nameless, difficult to understand, we, the prematurely born of a future as yet untested—for a new end we need a new means: a new health, a stronger, shrewder, tougher, bolder, gayer health than any the world has ever seen.

F. Nietzsche, *The Gay Science*

In 1938, Schwebkowski was taken out of Grade 6 and placed in the National Socialist Institute for Political Training at Ballenstedt, NAPOLA for short. The normal continuity of discipline in the home, grade school and high school was interrupted. A number of such ahistorical persons grew up in various NAPOLAs scattered throughout Germany, including Schwebkowski from 1936 to 1942. In 1943, Schwebkowski joined the Peter Freytag Division of the SS which was being organized in northern Greece. In the process of being assembled, however, the cadres of this division were reassigned to three army divisions. The immediate restoration of these divisions was given top priority; they were to be thrown into the threatened southern Ukraine—without the SS division. During his training, Schwebkowski quarrelled with an army officer. He escaped from the military prison because he faced the possibility of execution. In the uniform of a first lieutenant, he attached himself to army transports and crossed the Balkans, heading north. His original plan had been to get through to his old school in Ballenstedt. But since the number of military police increased as the troop trains in which he was travelling approached the old Austrian frontier, he slowed his journey in Laibach and continued on by other trains towards the south-east.

In the autumn of 1943, Schwebkowski met Francesca B. in Sofia, in a Romanian army billet. Schwebkowski became involved in business deals. When the Russians appeared in Sofia in 1944, Schwebkowski, who had taken off his uniform of a first lieutenant, was denounced by business friends. As a result, he lost B., whom he never saw again. He was taken to the transit camp not far from Odessa. To a rootless person such as Schwebkowski, the countryside cannot mean as much as it does to previous generations, for there is no piece of land that Schwebkowski wishes to own; and without the urge to ownership, there can be no pleasure in a beautiful landscape. This void is filled by one's relationship to the part of the country in which personal decisions have been made. The countryside between Kilomea and Odessa is therefore one of two homes for Schwebkowski, because one of two decisions affecting his life took place here.

Today Schwebkowski regards his decision in the spring of 1945 to escape from the transit camp near Odessa and get through to the legendary American lines in Kärnten as a wrong one. In retrospect, he feels his chances would have been better had he adjusted himself to prison work. In that case, he might have been back in Sofia before 1948, possibly as a Russian or Romanian citizen. Until that time, he would have found B. still living in Sofia.

II

Let us chase those Heaven-darkeners,
World-obscurers, cloud-gatherers,
Let us brighten the Empyrean!
Let us roar—O spirit
Of free spirits,
My happy soul roars like
The storm itself.

F. Nietzsche, *The Gay Science*

In 1945, many young people were looking forward to a splendid freedom, a new beginning. In June 1945, the commander of an American armoured division heading back west had set up headquarters in Halle. His measures kept the local authorities on their toes. Thanks to him, a teacher-training college opened in Halle as early as June 1945. The courses continued even when the Russians occupied Halle. It was at this college that Schwebkowski received his training. His hopes in the boundless possibilities of a teaching career were still intact. He took it for granted that the easiest way to regain the lost dream of the years 1936 to 1942 was as a teacher. From 1946 to 1949, Schwebkowski taught in the Halle and Magdeburg areas. In 1950, he accepted a teaching post at a private school in the south-west of the Federal Republic of Germany. In 1952, the school board in Freiburg discovered that all Schwebkowski had was some kind of wartime matric and a 1946 high-school teaching diploma which, according to the regulations laid down by the Ministry of Cultural Affairs, could not be recognized. His appointment was revoked. But this did not cause Schwebkowski to abandon his plan. He registered as a student at the University of Marburg. Marburg-on-the-Lahn is a serpentine town coiled round a hill. It is hemmed in by a serpentine highway leading along the valley of the river Lahn from Kassel in the north to Giessen in the south. Steep slopes on both sides prohibit detours, but permit walks. Schwebkowski sought to alleviate the dreariness of study by taking up music, but the lost dream of the years 1936 to 1942, which is a living thing, is not to be replaced by an evening at the piano. Dagmar Grothusen, a married woman, tried, so to speak, to lure Schwebkowski into a ravine. She saw a chance of utilizing his strength to bring about a change in her matrimonial captivity. She probably counted on Schwebkowski helping her if she relied on him sufficiently. It is difficult to escape such a situation when it occurs in desolate surroundings and with no hope for the foreseeable future. Only the conviction that a teaching career could restore something of the lost NAPOLA era induced Schwebkowski to invest so much in his studies. From what was a meaningless embrace, Frau Grothusen released Schwebkowski too late. Frau Grothusen did not want to have an abortion. Schwebkowski would have provided the funds from those he had just received from an inheritance. In order to escape the tiresome demands of this woman, Schwebkowski transferred to Munich and there obtained his teaching diploma.

III

In those days, every available new teacher in Bavaria, whether primary, vocational or secondary school, was sent to the Aschaffenburg area, where there was an acute shortage in every category. The proximity of the province of Hesse, which enjoyed a greater potential of new teachers, pointed up a certain deficiency in Bavaria's educational system. Schwebkowski found himself among the teachers provisionally assigned to this area. He had to do some probationary teaching in a number of schools, sometimes in the presence of a member of the school board who would assist him with advice. In Schwebkowski's background, the cogwheel of discipline was missing. Clashes with authority ensued here just as they had during his military training in northern Greece. In Schwebkowski's opinion, the preparatory period at university and the probationary period in schools were too long drawn out. He was also coming to believe less and less that his investment was balanced by even the slightest hope. After receiving his final diploma, Schwebkowski moved to the North Rhineland and Westphalia area where (with greater territorial scope) he hoped for more favourable working conditions. From 1958 to 1960, he taught in various schools in that region. He gathered impressions, found little to look forward to, but did not abandon his earlier hopes. In 1960, he met de Martin, Chief School Administrator, and a friendship sprang up with that busy man who was provided with an official car. De Martin tried to talk Schwebkowski into joining the Department of Education.

The aspirations Schwebkowski cherished and wanted to put into practice as a teacher were regarded by de Martin as utopian, even somewhat fascist. He pointed out that Schwebkowski never used the term National Socialist or National Socialism—he spoke either of Hitler or Fascism. Schwebkowski had still not adjusted, he was still animated by the rhythms of the years 1935 to 1945. De Martin did his best to persuade him. After Schwebkowski changed—from a schoolboy to a National Socialist, from a National Socialist to an aspirer after freedom, from an aspirer after freedom to an undergraduate, from an undergraduate to a conformist (so far always lured on by one goal)—he found himself face to face with someone who denied that a single one of the things he had stood for was real. Schwebkowski did not believe him.

IV

In autumn 1961, every teacher in D. was deeply shocked by Willett's arrest. Willett, who taught Latin, Greek and History, was the same age as Schwebkowski. Late one afternoon, he had been seen in a deserted map room of Grillparzer High School in the company of a young girl, 16-year-old P. Gnade. Nobody could offer a satisfactory explanation for their presence in the rarely used room; the statements of both pupil and teacher remained ambiguous. The school board tried to make light of the incident and suppress discussion of it by teachers in the city. The girl's parents, however, lost no time in filing suit. Before the case could come to trial, Schwebkowski managed to get his friend Willett, whose passport had been confiscated by the police, to Italy. But Willett, who had no training in escape methods, was arrested in Florence and extradited to the Federal Republic of Germany. Had Willett really committed an offence? For Schwebkowski (and for his champion de Martin, who was trying to win him over), this was completely irrelevant. Naturally, they denied the facts as presented by police and parents; but quite apart from that, an altogether different principle was involved: whether they were in a position to protect one of their own in an awkward dilemma such as this. It was a question of power, of whether education is a power, of whether protection is possible for education as a body.

V

Conversation with de Martin

> *The scientific principles which are the source of the individual maxims of school administration are kept constantly in mind by the School Board, and it serves the department by being able to supervise and properly appreciate its various methods along general lines; moreover, it performs those of*

the department's duties which require free time for scholarship and which cannot flourish amid the distractions of day-to-day business.

Wilhelm von Humboldt

The telephone in the chief administrator's office was busy through the morning. There was a short time when it was free, but then the school switchboard was overloaded. When Schwebkowski was able to dial his friend's office during the lunch hour, the secretary, who did not know who Schwebkowski was, told him de Martin had just left. Unnerved by the dialling and the long wait (at times he had used public telephones), Schwebkowski omitted to satisfy himself personally that de Martin was not in. If he had done so, he would have found the chief administrator still in his office.

In the afternoon, Schwebkowski was told that de Martin could be found in the parliament building. Schwebkowski looked for him the building where the Provincial Ministry of Cultural Affairs was in session. However, de Martin was engaged in conveying the greetings of the Minister of Cultural Affairs and the mayor to a teachers' conference elsewhere. Time was running out for Schwebkowski. He finally met de Martin that evening in the lobby of the Rhine Hall. As soon as de Martin saw his friend, his expression turned into a friendly grimace; he was well known for the speed of this transformation process: one moment a certain ministerial superiority, next the kind and helpful expression of a friend. He was still hoping to recruit Schwebkowski to the Department of Education. That was why he promised to speak to Deputies Fuhr and Semmler about the Willett case. Then De Martin ran into friends who were more important than Schwebkowski. Later, at the reception, he spoke to the above-named deputies; but since de Martin had a number of more urgent matters to discuss, he did not concentrate on the Willett case; the deputies almost immediately forgot the name. Though even if de Martin had made a greater effort, the outcome would presumably have been no different. That is probably why de Martin did not concentrate sufficiently on it. However, in order to utilize the slim chance of a stroke of luck in the Willett matter (e.g. that the district attorney's office would drop the case) to help him win over Schwebkowski, he did at least briefly mention the case, so as to be able to say he had spoken to Fuhr and Semmler about it, for de Martin habitually spoke the truth in such matters, since untruths lead to needless entanglements. The next day, Schwebkowski was unable to reach de Martin: he had gone on a tour of inspection to Münster, Cologne, Duisburg and Essen, and was not expected back until the end of the week. De Martin left a message with his secretary: he had spoken to the deputies. De Martin could not be reached while he was away. It did not take long for Schwebkowski to grasp the fact of de Martin's inaccessibility.

Willett Is Handed Over at Brenner Pass

Could the Austrian border officials have prevented the transit of the prisoner Willett from Italy to the Federal Republic? The Austrian colonel in charge of the border checkpoint at Brenner Pass advised against it. Opposite him sat Willett, wearing a shabby raincoat, exhausted from the strain of travelling under guard. Schwebkowski, who had arrived at the border during the night, tried to save his friend. But a refusal to permit the transit would merely have resulted in the return of the prisoner to Milan. From there, Willett would have been flown to Germany. The expenses of the flight would have had to been borne by Willett. The Austrian border officials could not save Willett either.

The Example of Ambassador von O.

In the Third Reich, there was a certain Ambassador von O. who later helped salvage the art treasures of Rome. He was not a National Socialist. But the position he held was of use to the National Socialists. He held it so as to be able to continue protecting friends and colleagues. His signature, his personality, his secret opposition, sheltered the policy of the National Socialists. In the end, he lost most of his friends and protégés, later even his post. After the war, he was court-martialled. The ambassador's permanently trumped-up position is a prototype for Schwebkowski; it indicates the borderline: as soon as it is no longer possible to protect one's friends, the time has come to change jobs.

Brief Summary

> *As water is conducted along a strand of wool from a full glass into an empty one.*
>
> Socrates

The educational methods of a society which does not truly desire education: 14 subjects are spread over 9, maximum 12 years. Everything is repeated twice. What is learnt at home is repeated in class. What is learned in three months is tested at intervals. If you pay attention, you get through without a scratch.

The Pedagogue Humbled by the Customs

In 1918, the Soviet teacher Makarenko, with by a group of eight juvenile delinquents, occupied a remote former-Tsarist barracks in which there was nothing but an axe which they could use to kill each other. They did not do so because they needed one another.

Returning to Berlin from a class outing with his pupils, Schwebkowski got into an argument with the West German Customs officials at

Helmsted. He had allowed the boys to take along papers and books printed in East Berlin. The Customs officials confiscated these; under the sharp eyes of the boys, who missed nothing, the teacher proved no match for ignorant officials. Copious correspondence later ensued, as the jurisdictional aspects of Schwebkowski's resistance could not immediately be clarified. In another instance, the school board objected to a class of 16-year-olds reading Jean-Paul Sartre's *The Wall.* In yet another instance, an outing promised by the teacher was not approved because of the risk involved in transporting the boys, the permissible quota of student accidents in that district having exceeded the maximum level. Because he could foresee similar obstacles, Schwebkowski refrained from even suggesting a considerable number of other projects.

Will the Teaching Profession Ever Become the Leading Profession?

> *All these elements: scholarly distinction, excellent professional standards, a commensurate salary, an outlook based on an innate dignity, combined with the considerate treatment accorded the teaching staff, have surrounded this profession with a respect and recognition in society which it had not hitherto possessed and which redounds very much to its advantage. Hence a young, well-qualified secondary-school teacher is, socially speaking, perfectly secure, he is at par with civil servants of other categories, even the most highly respected, and every year offers examples of marriages between such teachers and daughters from the families of the highest-ranking civil servants.*
>
> Friedrich Thiersch
>
> *Public Education* I, p. 460 (*c.*1840)

In practice, the position to which modern social developments entitle the teacher meets with considerable difficulties. A teacher lacks the freedom to shape his life in a manner in keeping with his function in society, and the independence and freedom of choice a treasury official has is far greater these days than that of a school teacher or principal. If senior civil servants and army officers represented the highest social level in the state at one time, it might be said that today, to use the metaphor of a bygone mode of thought, the teaching profession has attained the highest social level in the modern world.

Hellmut Becker
Quantity and Quality (1962)

Qualified teachers are paid according to the same scale as university laboratory assistants—what is the connection between the teaching profession and a civil-service salary scale? Teachers need a sabbatical year every seven years in order to bring themselves up-to-date—who gives them this free time? The problem of education, and thus of teacher training, is the greatest political concern of our time—but how many people take these matters seriously? The teaching profession needs dedication—but is it permitted to have it?

Quest over Which Willett Tripped

Narrow, brown back—not inviting to sexual intercourse. Bony and shivering under the skin—attractive to the initiated, moving to teachers. This was also destroyed many centuries ago in the Albigenses. The door to the seldom-used map room was flung open by the witness and subsequent informer: no power in the realm of culture can save the exposed teacher now.

Schwebkowski Abandons a Faith

The Willett case fully convinces Schwebkowski of something of which he was only partly convinced before—that the society in which we live has no use for education, for invention, for intellectual activity and quest. If this were not so, certain forces would come into play which could be employed in Willett's favour.

Development Since 1800

> *Are you not conscious in such figures as Spinoza, for example, of something profoundly enigmatic, puzzling and mysterious? Do you not see the drama being played out here, the steady draining of colour—the ever-more ideally interpreted desensualization? Do you not sense in the background some long-concealed vampire who begins with the senses and is finally left with, finally leaves, dry bones?*
>
> F. Nietzsche, *The Gay Science*

Around 1,800 apprehensive people started channelling Germany's intellectual life. Ideality replaced power, sublimation replaced criticism, legal history outdistanced law, attention was focused on philosophy rather than practice, on history of art rather than construction. Hegel was summoned to Berlin by the government to divert young people's minds from dangerous practical ideals. The pacification was successful. Of what use is a rebellion of the intellect when organized intellect opposes rebellion? Docile faculties let themselves be bullied and staffed by pacifiers who became pacified themselves; schools organized along military lines trained the non-commissioned officers and officers who won the battles of Königgrätz and Sedan and lost them between 1914 and 1918. What can the years of democratic work from 1923 to 1928 (preceded by inflation, followed by economic crisis) achieve against a hundred and fifty years of tradition? How quickly can tradition blot out a momentary hiatus in history between 1933 and 1945? Under the circumstances, Schwebkowski decided there was no point in being a teacher.

VI

Compromise is no basis for education, for education demands courage and resolution: its purpose is to give a direction to life.

Rahmenplan, p. 33

The final conversation between the two friends Schwebkowski and de Martin had to be postponed several times because of de Martin's heavy schedule. It took place at de Martin's home. De Martin had suggested this so he could exert his purely personal influence on Schwebkowski, in the hope that Schwebkowski's dissatisfaction with a teaching career might prompt him to join the Department of Education. He enticed him with visions of a higher salary scale. Frau de Martin served tea and joined in the attempt at persuasion.

In the spring of 1962, Schwebkowski changed careers. He joined a Düsseldorf real-estate firm. Here he was finally able to put to use the money he had received from his inheritance.

AN EXPERIMENT IN LOVE

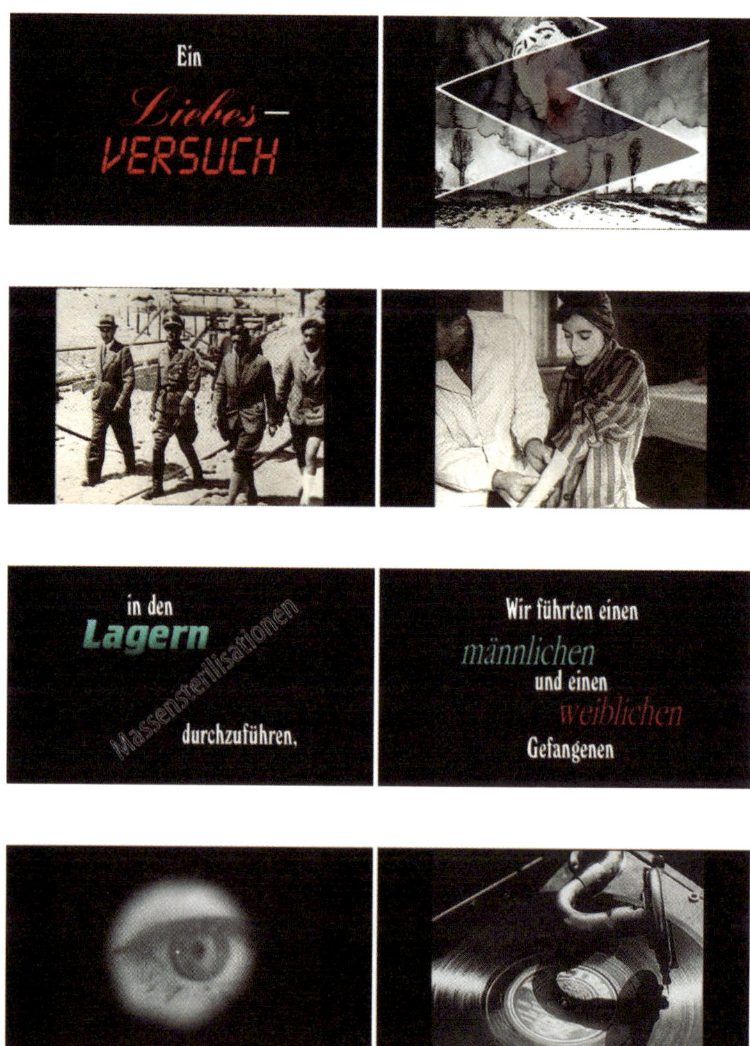

Stills from the short film *An Experiment in Love*. Premiered at Cinémathéque française, Paris 2013.

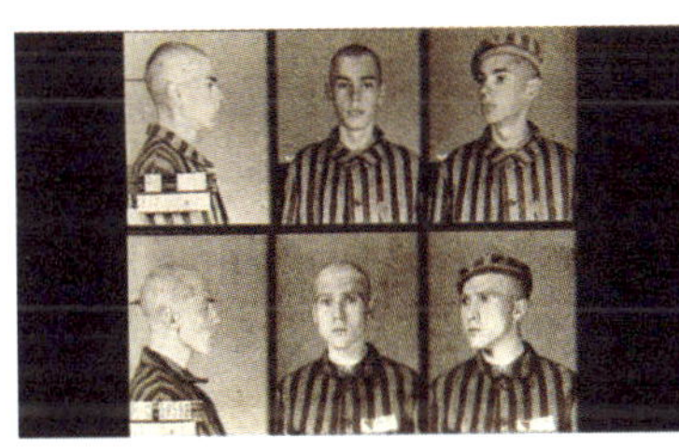

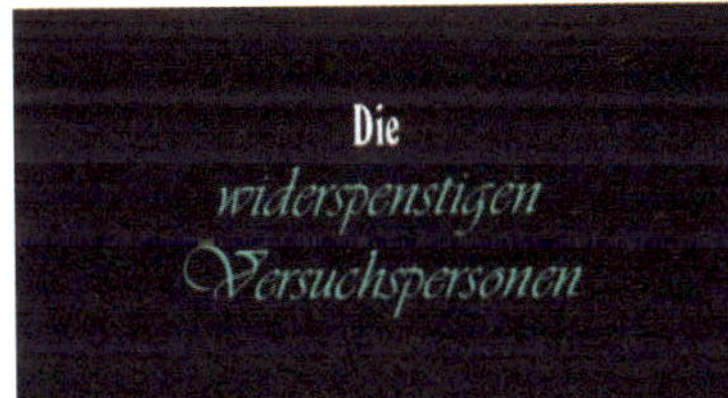

wurden
erschossen/

Bericht über ein
FORSCHUNGS-
ERGEBNIS

In 1943, the cheapest method of carrying out mass sterilization in the camps appeared to be the use of X-rays. There were some doubts as to whether or not the infertility thus achieved was of a lasting nature. We brought a male and female prisoner together for an experiment. The room provided for the purpose was larger than most of the other cells, and rugs from camp headquarters covered the floor. Hopes that in their nuptially furnished cell the prisoners would comply with the requirements of the experiment were not fulfilled.

Were They Aware They Had Been Sterilized?

Presumably they were not. The two prisoners sat down in opposite corners of the comfortably carpeted room. It could not be ascertained through the port hole, especially designed to provide surveillance, whether they had spoken to each other since being brought together. In any case, they did not converse. This passiveness was particularly undesirable because some high-ranking visitors had expressed their intention of watching the experiment; in order to expedite matters, the camp's medical officer in charge of the experiment gave orders that the prisoners' clothing be removed.

Were the Subjects Embarrassed?

The subjects could not be said to appear embarrassed. Generally speaking, they remained, even without clothes, in the same positions as before and seemed to be asleep. Let's wake them up a bit, said the doctor. Phonograph records were brought. It could be observed that the prisoners reacted to the music at first. Before long, however, they lapsed into their apathetic state. It was important the subjects get started, since that was the only way of ascertaining whether the unobtrusively induced infertility remained effective for prolonged periods. The staff members associated with the experiment waited in the passage a few yards away from the cell door. On the whole, they were quiet; they had been instructed to communicate only in whispers. There was always one observer at the port hole. The prisoners were to be lulled into believing they were now alone.

Nonetheless, the cell remained devoid of erotic tension. Those in charge almost believed that a smaller room would have been more suitable. The experimentees had been carefully selected. According to the files, the subjects could not fail to experience considerable reciprocal erotic interest.

How Did They Know This?

J., daughter of a senior civil servant in Brunswick, Jewish, born 1915, i.e. 28 years of age, married to an Aryan, matriculated, studied history of art, was regarded in the small town of G., in Lower Saxony, as the constant companion of the male subject, one P., born 1900, occupation: none. On account of P., J. left the husband who could have protected her, although she was a Jewess. She followed her lover to Prague, thence to Paris. In 1938, it became possible to arrest P. on Reich territory. A few days later, J. turned up on Reich territory in search of P., and was likewise arrested. In prison and later in camp, the couple made several attempts to meet. Hence our disappointment: now at last they were free to do it, and now they did not want to.

Were the Subjects Uncooperative?

They were obedient. I would say, therefore: cooperative.

Were the Prisoners Well Fed?

For some time before the start of the experiment, the subjects had been fed an especially nutritious diet. Now they had been lying for two whole days in the same room without making any discernible attempt to approach each other. We gave them the whites of fresh eggs to drink—the prisoners drank the albumen eagerly. Group Leader Wilhelm had them sprayed with garden hoses, after which, shivering with cold, they were conducted back to their comfortable room, but even the desire for warmth failed to bring them together.

Were they afraid of the moral laxity to which they felt themselves exposed? Did they think this was a test of their moral rectitude? Did the fatality of the camp stand between them?

Did They Know That, in the Event of Impregnation, Both Bodies Would Be Dissected and Examined?

It is unlikely that the subjects knew or even suspected this. They had received repeated assurances of their survival from the camp authorities. It is my belief that they did not want to do it. To the disappointment of Group Commander A. Zerbst and his staff, who had come here for this purpose only, the experiment was a failure, since all measures, including force, produced no positive results. We pressed their bodies together, held them so their skin barely touched while the temperature was gradually raised, rubbed them down with alcohol, fed the subjects alcohol, red wine with egg, even meat, also champagne; we adjusted the lighting, yet none of this brought on erotic excitement.

Did We Really Try Everything?

I can vouchsafe that we tried absolutely everything. We had a group leader among us who knew something about such matters. He tried one thing after another, measures never known to fail. We could not, after all, go in there ourselves and try our luck, since that would have been a racial crime. None of our measures succeeded in producing erotic excitement.

Were We Aroused Ourselves?

More than the couple in the room, certainly; at least, that's what it looked like. But then that would have been against regulations. I do not believe, therefore, that we were aroused. We were agitated, perhaps, because the experiment was not working out.

If I love thee and surrender,
Com'st thou to me in the night?

There was absolutely no way of inducing a positive reaction in the subjects, and the experiment was therefore abandoned as inconclusive. It was later resumed with other subjects.

What Happened to the Subjects?

The recalcitrant subjects were shot.

Would this Indicate That, at a Certain Level of Misfortune, Love Can No Longer Be Generated?

KORTI

The justice system in the Third Reich is a murder-machine. Of all the organizations that lived on past 1945, it shows the most tenacious power to survive. The story of a district-court judge named Korti.

'Korti, Endless'. 'A human being equipped with their character-armour.'

I
Korti Enjoys Success

Sum Total

In the first half of 1960, Korti was, on the whole, successful. An unknown young woman insulted him in January 1960 by directing an obscene remark towards the bench. Korti, who at that time was sitting in the little pub reserved for the judiciary (across the hall of justice) with a small lager, managed to establish the woman's personal details. The police, however, were unable to find her later at the address he had given them.

The President

The building in which the current county court, district court, public prosecutor's and district attorney's offices, remand centre and a few other departments are housed was taken over from former military district headquarters in 1945. The president had no choice;

if it had been up to him, he would have opted for a different building than that monumental one begun in 1935. The large vaulted chambers, offices and corridors do not give any real sense of being bomb resistant (judging by the overall noise sensitivity, there is no way the ceilings are as strong as they look), nor are they adapted to the idea of the administration of justice, which should not be contained in cellar-like buildings. Despite these reservations, the president would have liked to gain more precise knowledge, a theory of the building. For a long time, he tried to obtain the construction documents, but they were locked away in the main state archives, had possibly even been transported to the document centre in Berlin. In the future, heating repairs or changes to the interior construction will be necessary, and the pipe system could only be determined from the aforementioned documents. The president hates a uniquely pragmatic approach (e.g. only finding out later whether a water or heating pipe has been cut through a wall).

On his way up the stairs, bailiffs greet the president, judges collegially nod hello (their judicial decisions are independent from the president; his jurisdiction is limited to the presidential administration and management of assessors).

The Bailiffs' Hall

One single typewriter slowly ticks away in the room which is divided into several sections by shelves and waist-high barriers. At the moment, eight bailiffs find themselves in this massive, riding-hall-like room, a refurbished courtroom next to the main entrance. Typists appear at the pigeonholes for the incoming mail of the various court divisions and deliver it too. The incoming mail is stamped at two tables provided for this purpose. None of the bailiffs talk, though Gronke slams his receipt stamp numerous times, one after the other, on the documents he has received.

There is a problem: a typist would like to recover a letter which landed in the incoming mail by mistake. It has, however, already been stamped. It is uncertain whether the letter can be returned. Haubig and Hoffmann are unaware of anything similar ever happening before. The president cannot be questioned for such a petty case. Against the young woman's wishes, the letter is read out. Its content makes clear that it is of a personal nature; on the other hand, the receipt stamp has already been issued. Allowing every letter already received to be reclaimed would be going too far. Therefore, the letter remains with the incoming mail, but is not forwarded: it is held in reserve instead. The young woman is told that she can make a copy of the letter. She is handed the letter for that purpose. And is allowed to use Officer Saremba's typewriter to do so.

Lift

Korti enjoys taking the newly installed lift very much. Particularly pleasurable are the mirrors one can look into when one is by oneself. The lift is pleasurably warm.

Korti at the Hearing

The offender and defendant, a teacher, refused to sign a declaration that softened the offence. He was afraid that his adversary, a philologist, would publish said declaration in the philological journals and thus, to a certain extent, be rehabilitated. The teacher would only sign the declaration if an overall description of the dispute written by him was also made the subject of the settlement. In the meantime, the parties' legal representatives raised the issue of costs. At 12 o'clock, Korti's patience was at an end. Those justice seekers who had been waiting outside for hours and who could hear him were terrified. Within a quarter of an hour, their affairs, too, were settled. And thus Korti was still able to enjoy his lunch at 12.30 in the canteen, with other members of the judiciary.

The Canteen Head

The judges, court staff and casual visitors result in a daily market of 160 persons. The president enjoys his supervisory duties by having soup in the canteen once a month. He is always very happy with the quality. The canteen lessee, a still rather pretty woman from Saxony, delights him with her conversation. She breezily leans her hips against the counter, brushes blonde hair off her forehead. Her large eyes are almost always laughing, the speed of all the processes in her face make one forget that the size of her eyes is due to the fact that the eyes of Saxon women generally protrude further from their sockets. The president allows himself to get caught up in conversation, for it gives him time to really check his meal, which, naturally, is probably better than those filling up all the other plates on all the other tables. In this respect, this government measure, too, like so many others, is in vain.

In addition to the president's right of examination, the Judicial Committee has an independent right of examination, which District Court Judge Korti directs. In the past, Korti was one of the canteen management's main opponents. But now he too belongs to the circle of people who are personally attached to the woman.

Her husband, whom she'd brought along with her from the eastern zone, travels the areas of Cologne and Aachen as general representative for a watch company. He is rarely in the city. On weekends, the couple withdraws to the hotels of the nearby wooded mountains, out of consideration for an underage daughter who shares their flat. Refreshed, the canteen lessee returns to work every Monday, sends her daughter to secondary school, runs the canteen. Her system of rule is based on targeted friendships. This nets her enough money, though it's not all that easy to take advantage of judges and court employes, as their income is fairly low.

Korti Is in a Better Position Than His Colleague Wiegand

In February 1960, Korti would not have wanted to change places with his colleague, District Court Judge Wiegand, who presided over the sessions of the court of lay judges for the letters A through K. Mr Wiegand found himself in the unpleasant position of having to adjudicate a case concerning Mr Berthold, the ministerial director in the Ministry of Justice responsible for the entire administration of justice. A traffic offence.

In just such a case, or rather, had Korti been presiding over the court of lay judges, he either would have reported ill and allowed someone else to represent him, or handed down an unexpectedly tough sentence, though one with very weak justification. In that case, the court of appeals would have overturned it and, judging from experience, sentenced the offender leniently or acquitted him. Being acquitted or receiving a mild sentence from Korti himself would not have had the same result—the public prosecutor's office would have appealed, and the criminal division would have overturned the verdict and imposed a harsh sentence.

Korti would have made the senior official aware of this situation through intermediaries and also exclude the press from the hearing. District Court Judge Wiegand took a different approach. During the main hearing, he attempted to penalize the ministerial director who was his superior; the press was also present. Wiegand should have considered the fact that it wasn't a good idea to act as a judge, over a trivial matter, with a high-ranking civil servant who was also a politician, nor in the presence of the press. As a result, Wiegand created an enemy for himself, which one should only do if one is sure that one can really destroy the opponent in question.

Korti and the President

In March 1960, the president attempted several times to implement a new case-assignment plan among the various gentlemen of his judicial district. With Korti too, he tried to achieve changes. In return for taking some of the juvenile-court cases away, he hoped to give him the criminal-case letters S, T, U, V and W but in his capacity as a single-court judge. Naturally, Korti refused:

> To
> The President
> of the District Court in S.
>
> Dear Herr President!
>
> To my regret, I do not see myself in a position to accept the intended case-assignment plan in your decree of 10 October 1960. I have been focusing my special efforts on youth-oriented practice in the field of juvenile law for years. I would be reluctant to give up my jurisdiction, with which I have rather long and extensive experience. Were I to retain this jurisdiction, however, it would seem inappropriate for me to be additionally entrusted with the letters S, T, U, V and W as a single judge, for this would put me at a disadvantage compared to colleagues of the same rank and age. You can see from my roster how busy I have been in recent years. I am no different from other units in terms of points scored for cases processed over the last quarter. I would therefore ask you, Herr President, to refrain from placing an additional burden on me, which I have no choice but to perceive as a kind of assignment of punitive tasks.
>
> With the expression of my collegial esteem
> I remain your very loyal
> Korti

Had the president, following this letter, nevertheless persisted in his case-assignment plan, Korti would have filed a complaint with the president of the Higher District Court.

Korti and His Employer

As a juvenile magistrate district-court judge, Korti was not indisposed to a modern economic approach. In the proceedings against Jägerlein and Co., however, this point of view was not appropriate. The hearing revealed that not only Jägerlein, the accused juvenile, but also all employees of the timber wholesaler B. had damaged the company by unloading timber illegally (§ 242 StGB). The employer in the case of Jägerlein and Co. fought for his workers in the hearing from the unfavourable position of witness and plaintiff. To counteract the exodus of all his workers to prison, he resorted to making untrue allegations. Korti considered whether he should further damage the witness by swearing him in.

Following the hearing, the employer, having lost his workforce, got into his car in a rather depressed state. District Court Judge Korti is an independent judge who has no reason to fear any businessman.

Korti Doesn't Back Down from the Church Either

During the lunch break, Probation Officer Treiber turned up at the workplace of the young person entrusted to her care, K. She sent away the other girls who were still hanging around the office. She asked her probationer to help her move the office desks to the side. She knelt on the ground between the rather practical furniture and asked the girl to kneel down with her and thank the LORD for the work she'd been given. Later, they moved the tables back to their original places and waited for work to begin again. Given these interventions on the part of the probation service, that the young woman became a repeat offender was understandable. Korti considered it abusive for a church organization, a representative of such an organization or a person with other religious or ideological ties to exploit the dependency of a convicted person whose sentence had been suspended, that is, to hover over them like a sword of Damocles in order to satisfy their religious thirst. Emotionally (if not in terms of the offence), Korti equated such exploitation with fornication with addicts. For a moment, he wavered as to whether he should cancel the probationary conditions altogether, risking a conflict with his colleague Jakob. Instead, he decided to provide the convict with a new probation officer. (Miss Treiber, however, later found ways to get hold of the girl by standing in for Fehn, the girl's new probation officer, who was ill.)

Korti Puts the Railway Police in Their Place

In his capacity as a magistrate of the remand centre, Korti immediately summoned the newcomer brought in that morning by the railway police.

The remand centre was a barracks-like brick building with crenels that opened to the sky. The outside had some brick decoration, but it wasn't intended for the prisoners who could only have seen it if they had tried to escape, nor for passers-by, as outsiders were not allowed to enter the prison yard; it was only for the judges and clerks, whose windows looked out onto the courtyard. Small brick tunnels brought the prisoners from this building over to the court. That morning, Korti was still wide awake. At 9 already, he had enquired about new files; there weren't any. Everything had been processed, the docket next to him was empty. It was in this state that Korti became aware of the recent arrival. As he mistrusted the railway police on basic principle, he ordered the officers to appear regardless of the fact that they had been on night duty and were already in bed.

Questioning of the detainee:

Did you pay for the beer?

Yes.

The officials came and told you to finish it off?

To finish off my beer.

And then?

I slowly finished off my beer.

And the officials?

Returned before I'd completely finished.

How much was left?

(He shows how much)

Can the barman attest to this?

He's not going to get into it with the railway police.

Korti liked this response. Now he asked the officials.

Is that true?

Yes.

(To the second official, who hadn't said a thing:) And what do you have to say?

Likewise: Yes.

And so you arrested him?

Yes.

So why did the incident occur?

He resisted.

(This response angered Korti.) What did he do? Did he kick?

Korti had no doubt that the officials had acted without any reason. The officials maintained that the accused had referred to them as 'jackasses'. Korti's opinion on the matter had long been formed.

Korti Brings a Witness Down from the Rhine

In early May 1960, a pub landlord didn't want to appear for his hearing after having filed charges against the salesman Qu. for an unpaid tab in April 1959. Despite repeated lawful writs, on the day of the hearing, he was more interested in hosting a boat trip on the Rhine (featuring drinks and dancing), which had already been announced in the papers; he'd even rented and equipped a steamer for that very purpose.

District Court Judge Korti waited half an hour for the witness. At first, he could not imagine the witness tossing the summons—served on him personally, thanks to his signature being on the certificate of service (which could be established by comparing the signatures on the complaint and the certificate of service)—to the wind. Once it had been established that the witness was not merely late, Korti initiated a police search.

The water police's quick boats set off looking for pub landlord K. on the Rhine between Eltville and Bingen. On that sunny, summer-like day, many pleasure travellers on the Rhine steamers were amazed at the excitedly cruising speedboats, spraying water at the front, subjecting various steamers to close observation. Just before the office closed at 4.30, police officers brought the witness to the hearing. Korti's questioning lasted five minutes. The defendant was sentenced to five days in jail. The costs of the proceedings as well as the police search were imposed upon the witness.

Judges are often underestimated because they receive a comparatively low salary. That is why Korti set an example. The misconception that one can mess with a judge with impunity must be corrected. Not even the injured party can do that.

Korti and the Police Quadrigas

In the winter of 1959, Korti was elected honorary chairman of the mounted police squadron in S. He was not a rider himself. Horses were foreign to him, and the idea that he could get somewhere more quickly by horse would have struck him as absurd. The estrangement went so far that Korti immediately associated the word 'riding' with sex rather than horses. The situation was different for the mounted-police squadron which had elected him honorary president. In May 1960, that is, during the year of his honorary presidency, Korti succeeded in getting the higher authorities of the internal administration to provide the squadron with the means to prepare two police quadrigas, a dapple grey and a grey one, that would be led from behind with four reins by a mounted police sergeant on a brown horse, which would temporarily replace the actual carriage of the quadriga. Korti managed to get the interior minister of his federal state to enforce the approval of funds. Then, at the police sports festival in the summer of 1960, the squadrons—welcomed by the press as well—were presented. First there were the obligatory motorbike tricks, dog demonstrations and police-squad rides. But then, all of a sudden, the two teams of quadrigas arrived. They circled the stadium three times before stopping in front of the stand of honour where Korti was sitting. The district-court president and the chief of police nodded to Korti as the quadriga stopped right in front of the stand. The two quadriga leaders in white police uniforms shouted something unintelligible up to the tribune; those in the tribune took it as thanks for having authorized the funds. 1960 was a good year for Korti. One success after another. These were the best years of his life, a certain self-respect combined with many years of experience, while his physical strength was yet to diminish. Korti was quicker than all his colleagues, more effective and prudent. Not to mention more democratic and modern.

Korti Deals with a Lay Judge

A certain Fräulein von Saalburg had decided to cross the street before hesitantly stopping in the middle and turning around. Thus stepping into the path of a lorry, whose only option was to swerve into a parked car. Obviously, the witness was just about blind, despite her glasses; during her appointment with Korti, an official had to turn her in the former's direction, and even then she couldn't see a thing. She couldn't recognize anything and could barely remember the incident; being for the most part unable to notice anything, she hadn't even been frightened. Korti assumed that the long-distance lorry driver would have to be convicted, as the owner of the parked car was obviously blameless and Saalburg could not be held responsible; a guilty party had to be named, not least because of the settlement of the insurance claims, which were otherwise hanging in the air, so to speak.

At noon, Korti interrupted the hearing for an hour. In the canteen, he could observe the still-very-young lay judge (her occupation had been listed as 'housewife' but to him she seemed more like a concubine), her beautiful face excited as she talked the other lay judges into acquitting the lorry driver. She covered her lay colleagues', the legal assessor's and the trainee lawyer's sausages and beer. Korti didn't want to intrude, especially as he hadn't been asked to take a seat at the table.

Did the young woman have a thing for the lorry driver? Could she not have imagined that Korti had enough *experience* to outplay her, even if, in her zeal for the accused, she managed to overrule the chairman (i.e. Korti) with the help of the assessors? In addition to the judges' excess of work, here women's whims come into play. Korti reluctantly let himself be overruled. When drafting his judgements, Korti considered the many peculiarities of the Grand Criminal Chambers (to which the appeal cases go) that he had observed.

For Korti, every appeal was an exam, he usually waited to dictate the reasons for a particular verdict until it was certain whether an appeal would be lodged; he fine-tuned those that went up the chain, week after week. Only rarely were Korti's well-established rulings overturned. Conversely, by the specific way in which a verdict was drafted, Korti could call one of the Grand Criminal Chambers into action against recalcitrant lay judges. His speculation in the case of this particular lay judge went in just such a direction: as to be expected, Grand Criminal Chamber II under Director Hoffmann was annoyed by Korti's inadequately justified acquittal of the lorry driver. The driver received several months in prison at the appeal. Korti sent the verdict together with a cover letter to the blonde lay judge, whose address was on record.

Korti's Superiors

The appeal cases are collected in the offices of the district court and brought to the third floor of the court building by bailiffs, where they are sorted into juvenile and adult criminal cases; the adult criminal cases are distributed by letter to two large criminal chambers. The head of Grand Criminal Chamber I is District Court Director Dr Friedrich. The head of Grand Criminal Chamber II is District Court Director Hoffmann.

Is Dr Friedrich Human Because He's Weak?

Many convicts consider Dr Friedrich to be a mild judge, as he sacrifices time for them, attempts to empathize with their destinies, in other words, he's curious, presumably human, too. He is often in pain; he must drink water and take tablets. He often has to interrupt hearings, which then extend deep into the night. Court ushers bring canapes and wine for the judges. Other convicts say that, yes, he does listen for hours, but he forgets everything thereafter. An inexperienced defendant can easily get caught up in the web of kindnesses that Dr Friedrich spreads about them and eventually lose sight of their goal to get out of there. Moreover, even the strongest defendant cannot hold out for a 10 hour trial, whereas Dr Friedrich, who eats and drinks in between, is at his best in the evening hours. Once convicted, the accused is then confronted with an administration of justice that is not curious, not dreamy, not humanly weak. In this respect, the result of Dr Friedrich's benevolence is rather inhuman.

Is Dr Friedrich an Intellectual?

Convicts say: Heaven protect us from an intellectual judge who is not really an intellectual. What good does it do us if they play piano but allocate the time at the end of the hearing so poorly that the deliberation results in a verdict based purely on mood? God protect us from a good human being if they have no staying power. What good is a day of amicable proceedings if there is no time in the evening to weigh up the guilt of the accused? The district-court president considers Dr Friedrich's sentencing style (we are referring here to his earlier sentences, as today Dr Friedrich no longer writes any sentences) classic; captured by Friedrich's excellent performance of Chopin on the piano, the president assumes that Friedrich has a comprehensive mind, just as many consider a nervous dentist who calms his nerves by playing the piano a genius; only numerous mistakes will destroy the myth. It is, however, impossible to prove mistakes in criminal practice, for who would judge them? Having said that, the office staff, who adhere to the sentencing statistics and know the files, see the limited scope of Friedrich's interests: he is mainly interested in defendants like himself; he feels, as it were, for those crimes in the hearings that he, in his high position, cannot himself commit.

Why Is Hoffmann so Ferocious?

For a period during the winter of 1959, many hoped—including the director of the administrative offices, the councillors, the assessors, the court reporter, the bailiffs—that Hoffmann would have a heart attack, become unable to work and die, but any such hopes were soon dashed. Hoffmann is a heavyweight, brown-eyed, careful, wide-faced man, who suffers from a weak heart and circulation; a great big bristly head above a short body and neck, his long cheeks turn red when he gets excited during interrogations of the accused, i.e. his cheeks turn reddish-blue, so that in addition to the moral and legal pressure of the trial, defendants are afraid of being guilty of the death of the presiding judge if they annoy him any further by resisting. There are harsh penalties.

Bad Blood between Hoffmann and the District Court President

In an argument between Director Hoffmann and his assessor, the president had to arbitrate when a lay judge, a primary-school teacher, threatened to leave the courtroom for being shouted at by the presiding judge simply for having raised a question. By order of the director, a bailiff held him at the door until the president could be summoned at the instigation of the public prosecutor who wanted to mediate. Director Hoffmann was sitting in an elevated chair, his cheeks blueish, his small, round, brown eyes aimed at the runaway assessor. The president asked the teacher into his office and managed to persuade the man to return to the bench. There, however, it turned out that the primary-school teacher's boss (i.e. Hoffmann), who'd shouted at him for not being able to express himself succinctly, had left in a rage without leaving a note at the office mentioning where he could be found. Now the president was annoyed, and dismissed the participants of the hearing who were still waiting. The defendant was returned to the remand centre.

Korti's Superiors in His Own Eyes

Korti feared Dr Friedrich's short, often incomprehensible innuendos in his direction; Director Hoffmann's unpredictability, his often irritable reactions to tactically successful points of view in the explanations for verdicts. Just why outsiders were made the guardians of the court of appeals was unfathomable to Korti. His suggestion: 40 assessors, freshly trained in expert opinion and judgement style. One day, Dr Friedrich invited Korti to a wine tasting with liverwurst in the Rheingau district. The whole evening Korti didn't feel too well. He thought that drinking a lot of wine would give him a greater sense of security, but all it did was make him feel queasy. He had to have the court's driver bring him home. Though this may have been a failure, it was offset by numerous successes in dealings with the Grand Criminal Chambers.

Emboldened by Half a Bottle of Champagne, Henderson Goes to See Hitler

England's ambassador Nevile Henderson, hoping to settle the Czech crisis in 1938, fortified himself with half a bottle of champagne before going to see Hitler. The champagne eased his nerves, made him confident of success, even superior to the dangerous Führer. Before dangerous undertakings Korti would have a shot of liquor or glass of brandy.

A Love Affair that Soon Dries Up Again

Prior to attending the company's Ascension Day get-together, Korti was feeling anxious. The little frequented party was a creation of the canteen lessee to increase her revenue; Korti brushed against the all-around admired woman. An attempt to nudge her while getting closer to her hand with his little finger while glasses were clinking in toasts. Which was unsuccessful, but the woman grabbed his hand and caressed it. After the president and district judges had gone, and only the tightest clique about the canteen lessee was left, they put on records. Korti led the lovely woman to a recess where they drank to each other's health.

Later, Korti found himself between this equally successful businesswoman's strong legs. After a time, the woman's underage daughter came into the room in a bathrobe. Until then, Korti had not known that she was even in the flat; she sat down on her mother's double bed. The women exchanged a few words. Korti asked, as soon as the girl left the room for a moment (to get a bottle of wine from the refrigerator), how old she was. The information frightened him, he didn't want to stay any longer. The canteen lessee had to drive him home. This experience confirmed her view that, with anxious types, there simply was no business to be done. She would have liked to see Korti obligated as a precautionary measure for the small increase in canteen prices. The next day, Korti appeared at lunchtime as if nothing had happened. He seemed to have forgotten the informal 'you' to which they had drunk. At that, the canteen lessee likewise forgot what had happened.

There's a Problem

The juvenile Slotosch proceedings concerned a case of incest between the older sister and her under-age brother. The family was originally from the east. What form of punishment was applicable to the young Slotosch?

Is Any Solution Possible?

Korti intended to go on holiday at the end of May. He could not find any appropriate form of punishment in the Slotosch case. He made a call to the principal of the Prinz-Max Gymnasium, who was familiar with it from the paper, but he was similarly at a loss of what to do. Korti toyed with the idea of having a temporary replacement assigned.

Found

June 1960! Korti was thinking about something and looked towards the window, and then thought that he, in fact, wanted to look out the window. Unexpectedly, he saw that very person (passing by the hall of justice) who in January had said: Just once in my life, I'd like to have a judge in between my legs. Thereafter, she had given a false address. Korti caught up with the insulter before she could step onto an omnibus. The surprised woman gave him her real address. Then was immediately sent a penalty. This was the day before Korti was to go on holiday: 1 June. No one gets away from Korti that easily.

II
Annihilation of the Enemy

Labyrinth

A few examples of cases that come up over the course of a year in Judicial District S.:

I

During the air raid of Dresden in February 1945, all of 14, the now 29-year-old, twice-convicted W. found himself in the city reformatory housed in the spaces of the city prison. During the night attack, the prisoners had already begun to destroy their cells in fear: the prison one big, open noise-wound. At the beginning of the second attack in the morning, the guards opened the cells indiscriminately. The prisoners killed some of the latter before scattering along the banks of the Elbe, where some of them were pursued in turn by enemy fighters. W., too, joined the escapees. This was a mistake insofar as everything that followed was based on this—perhaps reckless—initial move.

Later, W., aged 16, committed robberies in the West. He shot two police officers who were supposed to transport him in a car from Wiesbaden to Munich with the service pistol he'd stolen from one of them. The courts were initially unable to understand the implausible course of events, and later sentenced W. to a Bavarian prison. He served 10 years. During this time, hope began to gather. The bleak years of prison life allow a reversal of opinion as to how great freedom can be. Released from prison, W. fell into the hands of a prison carer who had already shown her kindness to numerous prisoners. At this point, W. could have taken up any of several professions, pioneering professions. He would have liked to go to Abyssinia, South America or Antarctica, but, being on probation, he couldn't get the necessary papers. He wasn't interested in atonement, for—seeing as they were enemies—he did not regret his killing of the two police officers (although it had become a habit to talk about atonement in prison). He worked at a laundry. Caught in the crossfire between his caretaker's charity, being on parole and the burden of work, he sought refuge with the wife of a prison officer. After a while, W. was taken by surprise while attempting another burglary. He received a prison sentence of two and a half years and his suspended juvenile sentence, the five years in prison remaining from the police murder, was reinstated: he was to go to prison for seven years. Which is he to serve first: the newly imposed prison sentence of two and a half years or the suspended prison sentence of five years, which has since been revoked?

2

A girl who finds life with her parents, her family, impossible. Unable to handle seeing the vulgarity of her loved ones, she decides to kill them. She shoots her beloved brother; a nervous breakdown keeps her from killing the others. What kind of sentence is possible?

3

Dr S. is a hard-working, educated, good-looking physician. Once, during the war, he made himself available as a senior physician in a field hospital just to highlight the untenable conditions and lack of care; this was immediately remedied by the superior authorities. For years now, this physician has run a private clinic; it is small because S. attaches importance to utmost precision, caution and technical exactitude. On the day of his offence, he was wide awake, had slept well, no unfavourable influences upon body or spirit. From his statement: The patient complained about pain on the right side of her stomach. Examination revealed powerful tension and sensitivity to pain precisely there. All symptoms pointed to appendicitis. But during the operation, we were unable to find the small intestine. In the area where it should have been, I found a yellowish fluid, which I soaked up with the swab. Following the operation, the patient slept peacefully for hours. But during the night the fever vigorously increased, and the responsible night nurse called me at my private home. Now, during the operation we hadn't found any inflamed appendix or significant inflammation at all; I was certain that there was no inflammation. I went over to the clinic and examined the patient, who had a strong and, to me, utterly inexplicable fever. The whole night long I ruminated about what could be wrong. At 7 a.m. I called Prof. H. at the university hospital. I urged him to admit the woman. During my morning consultation hours, I tried several times to speed up the process.

I then heard from the receptionist that the ambulance had arrived, so went over to supervise the transfer. All the nurses were in the room. There was a great state of alarm. I was certain that there was no inflamed small intestine to be found. But then my office hours completely absorbed me. Later, I drove to the hospital. But I could not find Frau X for the life of me. My bedside visits and a subsequent urgent operation kept me busy throughout the afternoon. At the university hospital in the evening, I only managed to reach the senior physician, who spoke of a second operation on Frau X., which the head physician had performed, and that the patient now had no fever. I thought to myself: Now everything is fine, it looks as if I overlooked a case of inflammation after all. Please call me, I said to the doctor, if anything happens. The whole of the following day I didn't hear a thing. But when I ended up calling in the late afternoon, I learnt that Frau X had died. The information provided by the senior physician about a second operation was based on an error: it referred to another person whom the physician had confused with Frau X. An autopsy was performed on Frau X's corpse that same day: two small injuries in the vicinity of the small intestine. In retrospect, I could not get rid of the thought that it would have been better for me to keep the patient and operate a second time. But would I have found the injuries? The prosecution brought charges against me, assuming that I was the one who could have caused the woman's injuries. The public prosecutor told me that, although he did not believe in this possibility himself, he was a layman and the question had to be clarified because an individual life is no trifling matter. I agree with him, even when I would not express it the same way.

What is the appropriate punishment?

4

Jordan, Mahlke and two police officers are standing before the court. They had served as gendarmes in the Upper Silesian district capital of Grottkau in January 1945. At the approach of the Russians on 30 January 1945, they appeared at St Joseph's Hospital, Ottmachau, which was run by Catholic nuns and filled with the mad. Against the resistance of the nurses, who, however, did not recognize the gendarmes' intentions, they had auxiliary officers pour two bottles of poison into the patients' tea, which resulted in two deaths. Disguised as the heads of the Red Cross, Jordan and Mahlke appeared again the following day—the Russian advance had come to a temporary halt at the district border—to distribute larger quantities of a stronger poison to the patients. This time too, only a few of them died; the residents defended themselves against additional injections of poison by flocking together. The gendarmes were at a loss. They fetched the district party leader from Grottkau, who drove the inmates into the isolation house and shot them. Which is why he'd had the service weapons of the gendarmes and the accompanying policemen handed over to him. At that time, the nuns were being transported to Glogau.

Two years or fifteen, of prison time, for Jordan and Mahlke?

5

One day, the bicycle of watchman Heinrich F. of the Security and Lock company was stolen. A few days later, while on duty, F. noticed a young man tampering with a bicycle in a car park for which F. was responsible. F. became particularly agitated. When the youth did not respond to his call, F. fired his service weapon three times, hitting the youth in the stomach. The bullets injured the latter's liver and stomach in 11 places. The young man dragged himself along for about 250 metres before collapsing. F. did not go to check on his victim, as obliged to, nor did he inform the police, but continued on his way. What punishment is appropriate?

6

In 1936, the cafe owner L. was driven out of Germany by the National Socialists. In 1940, he left France for Portugal. From there, he made it to the island of Cuba. And waited for permission to enter the United States. The US, however, turned out to be a prison. Every time L. tried to get a coffeehouse going, he ended up entangled in debt, which he was only able to get free of after years of working as a waiter. Full of hope, in 1958, he returned to Germany. But he was unable to find any of his earlier friends. After closing, he invited one of the under-age girls working for him in his coffeehouse to his private office. His error consisted in attempting to lock the door. His first attempt at making a pass at another human being in 15 contactless years. The girl's parents naturally filed charges. L. understood things as follows: in 1936, the National Socialists were close to catching him directly; now, these people had caught him via the judiciary.

Where are the judges for these and similar cases?

A Devourer of Pigs' Ears

Dr Korti was eating a pig's ear, surrounded by vegetables. In that part of town on the other side of the river, where things like that were available. Some of the vegetables had come from Malta by air, the proprietor told him. Like a wide, stiff rag, the pig's ear lay on the plate, but with very tasty bits of meat hidden in its nooks and crannies. At meals, Korti allowed beer to flow into his stomach, not in sips but in distinctly long streams, which triggered a tingling in his throat that Korti only interrupted when it became too pronounced. He sat alone. In that somewhat twilit state, the pub's lamps large pinkish balls, Korti thought about his nemesis, Dr Glaube.

The Exception of Dr Glaube

For years, District Court Judge Dr Glaube had been waiting, cautiously, which made him quite popular with his colleagues on the board of appeals—in Civil Chamber IV of the district court of S.—for the case that was meant for him, one in which he would act and turn the law on its head, so to speak. A case big enough to justify the use of his entire person. Indeed, Dr Glaube's whole reason for being a judge was to be ready for just such a case. Over the years, Glaube had missed several chances which, only in retrospect, turned out to have been big. Thanks to his reserve, his mediating stance, Glaube is quite popular among his colleagues. If necessary, they would follow him some of the way; but maybe they would follow him so far that they would have to follow him all the way. A case big enough for Dr Glaube's intentions, he realizes, is not forthcoming. A comprehensive project like Dr Glaube's cannot be carried out in small change.

Glaube, born November 1917 in Schneidemühl (West Prussia). Protected by fate, that is, destined for big things. 1936 *Abitur*. 1941–43: lieutenant. No broken bones. No injuries of a mental nature. 1944: wartime judge in Paris. 1946: district judge in Flörsheim (on the Main). 1953–56: director of Prison B. in Hesse, which he reformed. A prison-break attempt (the guards had been warning about carrying out such liberal methods beforehand) cost him his position. 1956–62: employed at the district-court board of appeals in S. And then one day the long-expected case, the case of P., arrives.

The Case of P.

A girl with the surname P. is being held in the state sanatorium. It is believed that she stands a chance of being cured, though at considerable cost. Money would be available if a carer could be appointed for her to collect her claims for compensation. As a child, she watched a concentration-camp leader rape and kill her young mother, or possibly just kill her. Her story is unclear. Many experts consider the lack of clarity she shows in this matter, as in many others, and which is what brought her to the sanatorium, to be a consequence of her impressions at the time. Other experts point to the statistical experience that the number of psychoses does not increase even in times of emergency; for this reason, they conclude there is parallelism, but no causality. The dispute between the schools is complicated. In this respect, it is fortunate that the case does not come to trial and remains within the state sanatorium.

Dr Glaube in the Case of P.

It was clear that in the case of P. he had to do something, that he had to break the vicious circle, interrupt general satisfaction with the result obtained until then.

Bad Blood Between Glaube and His Fellow Judges

In view of the expert scientific opinions, many of S.' judges found the decision of the Board of Appeals to release P., who had been committed, and to send the files to the Restitution Chamber, questionable enough. Which is why the Higher Regional Court had also overturned the decision. And so Dr Glaube adopted the girl, who had already been returned to the sanatorium, demanding her return by virtue of parental rights. An open snub to the Higher Regional Court ruling. Dr Glaube subsequently paid the patient's considerable medical costs out of his own pocket. P.' s claims for restitution had been dismissed with final effect, in accordance with the expert opinions of renowned university professors. Overall, Glaube's behaviour is incomprehensible.

Korti and the Case of P.

He, Korti, did not have anything to do with the case. No one could have stood in the way of Glaube adopting the girl, as everyone is free to conclude legal transactions. *It is a different question entirely whether it was right to become set on P. and to snub the Higher District Court!*

Korti at the Cafe

Korti was sitting in a cafe: at about 2 metres away, there was a woman cutting up her cake, eating it and meeting Korti's gaze, which he had only allowed to sweep over her in passing. The skill Korti employed (the random gliding of his eyes) could seem ridiculous given the openness with which she looked at him. Korti glanced past her into the street. Suddenly he heard a giggling, the woman, high small breasts, went to get a paper. She didn't speak, nor read through the paper; no, she stared straight at him, Korti, so there was no way for him to avoid her glance. The result: a grimace. The woman was wearing a lucky die around her neck, right where a guillotine would have cut through it. Korti said: Your die is like a medal. Her face contorted. Later she stood up and said something Korti that did not understand. Pulled money out of her coat. The waitress wanted to hand her some change, but the woman was having none of it. Korti decided to follow her. He too paid and told the waitress to keep the change. He followed the woman. She took the high street to Opernplatz at a comfortable pace; later he lost sight of her. Had she climbed onto a bus?

Annihilation of the Enemy

Most judges in S. considered it possible that Glaube had inappropriate relations with P. What counted against Glaube was the fact that he had stood up so radically for the girl. This was aggravated by the fact that P., who had only been released from the sanatorium by means of a trick, was still to be regarded as restricted in her free will (§ 176 II, number 2 StGB). When suspicions to this effect were raised by colleagues, the judicial disciplinary committee for the district of S. asked Glaube to attend an informal hearing. It was incriminating for Glaube that P., questioned about her attitude towards Glaube during the hearing, made a statement that could only be interpreted as a declaration of love. Under the impression of the growing suspicion surrounding him, after the informal hearing before the disciplinary committee, even before he had been investigated by the public prosecutor, Glaube attempted suicide, and this cost him his eyesight. In this state, he was no longer fit for judicial service.

P., domiciled in Glaube's flat, was re-admitted to the sanatorium in O. (Rheingau) while Glaube was still in hospital.

The chairman of the disciplinary committee that organized the informal hearing was District Court Judge Korti.

VICTORY LAP OF THOSE JUDGES WHO PARTICIPATED IN GLAUBE'S ANNIHILATION

A Sense of Justice Satisfied

> It would be interesting to learn how many spectators of an execution experienced disgust more than a satisfied sense of justice.
>
> *Letter to the Editor*

The satisfied sense of justice is the sound of the horn after a successful hunt. For the unbiased, the punishment cannot be any consolation for the crime. The feudal hunting lord is satisfied by the death of the poacher and the forest outlaw, he even forgets the occasion because he has taken a step forward in his struggle: the death is a precedent in his favour. Thus the death of the 16-year-old thief in 1700 satisfies the Hanseatic League. It is a precedent in its favour. The factory owner around 1900 is satisfied by the death of the murderer even after 10 years of waiting; the murder does not affect him, but the death of a murderer makes it clear that the factory owner's life is not to be touched. Today, the death of the traitor to the country and the constitution should be particularly satisfying to a general sense of justice. Church and property justice is followed by political justice as the last line of defence, not only of the Western world but of justice itself.

District Court Judge Jakob

A defender of the fortress of justice.

André Gide

Recollections of the Assize Court

Hallmark: Satisfied sense of justice.

Snapshot: With his large, full (if cut to stubble) head of hair, Jakob sits upon the bench, one eye cocked at the clock at the top of the dark room, which like a goddess controls the even distribution of justice: Mondays and Tuesdays from 8 to 12. At 8 a.m. on the dot, Jakob enters the room, prepared for the day's hearings. A glance at the clock convinces him that the appointment scheduled for 8 can also begin on time. From 8 to 12, every quarter hour, District Court Judge Jakob casts it a glance, like a brief *Our Father*, as he divides the morning's events into units of 15 minutes each and sticks to this timetable, just as he notes the times at which the train passes certain stations when he travels by train or makes sure that his eight daughters, who will probably never find husbands, prepare the table at the right time and sit there themselves. Essentially, the only remnants of paternal authority are these communal meals; what remains of justice is order. Jakob punishes according to fixed ethical criteria: first of all, he uses maximum and minimum punishments as a basis. An additional three months is added for onanism, three months for adultery and three months for lying. Recidivist defendants have the option of being re-sentenced. Here you can still sense something of the original unity of the system.

District Court Judge Jakob isn't interested in minimizing the impact of crime, as this would also reduce the justice system's reputation. There's more to it: justice that is no longer applied on a large scale finds partial fulfillment in the interplay between justice and crime, a fulfilment that is no longer granted to it in society (though Jakob would have preferred large-scale solutions). The last time a large-scale solution would have been possible, however, was the French Revolution of 1789. General clumsiness brought down the revolution at its peak.

Participated Against Glaube: Because Glaube's method (not only in the case of P.) rocks the foundations of justice. Individual analytical methods (in other words: caprice) are as unbearable in the judiciary as, for example, they are in the construction of a communist state. Glaube's exit is regrettable, but necessary.

Rationale: The idea of justice has shrunk. Many see the judiciary as nothing more than a regulatory factor. This makes it all the more important to defend the fragments of an originally great idea. Through his example, Glaube undermined the institutions of justice without, as an individual, being in a position to replace them with something appropriate to justice. Fortunately, Glaube had got caught up in his own machinations, i.e. he maintained unauthorized relations with his adopted daughter.

Whether that has been proven?

Breustedt says it has. In any event, suspicion is within the realm of possibility.

District Court Judge Breustedt

Hallmark: An uncontrollable desire to denounce.

Snapshot: As an artillery officer in an armoured division, Breustedt was captured by the Russians in 1943. 10 years spent in officers' camps have intensified the soldier's sharp facial features. Judge Breustedt looks as if he could only remain silent. In contrast to this is a need to communicate, a deformity acquired in captivity. Others come home with frozen limbs or brain injuries; Breustedt could be compared to a plane whose load has slipped forward and crushed the cockpit. If as an artillery officer, it had been his duty to recognize suspicious movements and report them upwards, in captivity it was necessary to keep abreast of developments but to watch his tongue; now the duties of a long soldier's life have shifted into one another: the hero's luminous eyes note suspicious trifles, suspicious trifles add up to suspicious factors, suspicious factors surge towards the tongue. The tongue cannot be stopped: Breustedt is incapable of not sharing. He is responsible for most of the gossip in the court in S.

Participated Against Glaube: Glaube offended the sensibilities of all moral thinkers.

Rationale: Glaube abused his adoptive daughter, P. The suspicion of an offence is based on the following considerations: (1) G. and P. lived (although neither married nor related by blood) in one and the same flat; (2) on a visit of Breustedt's to Glaube's, P. opened the door insufficiently clothed; (3) G. was at that time present in the flat; (4) during further conversation that evening, P. spoke to Glaube in an intimate manner; (5) general human experience; (6) special evaluation of Glaube's character and general outlook.

District Court Judge Wilke

The play-actor of his own ideal.

Friedrich Nietzsche
The Gay Science

Hallmark: Kind and liberal, but not consistently kind and liberal. Incapable of opposing others who are planning illiberal things. As a result, he belongs to the unkind, probably because he lacks the motive for kindness.

Snapshot: From the moment the judge had begun to address her informally, the defendant no longer answered. The judge needed a final word from her for the minutes. The defendant did not answer; the judge had to formulate it himself. The defendant asked for a lenient sentence. She received a lenient sentence. At the approach of a police siren, the defendant would have listened, someone coming up the stairs would have worried her, as it would mean that a police control was also coming up the stairs. She did not, however, take for granted the personal questions that Wilke put to her after the verdict. She didn't believe the judge's kindness, she thought it was his particular way of ensuring a good day. The judge was disappointed when his humanity found no response.

Participated against Glaube: Glaube committed a decisive error in not coming to terms with his colleagues.

Rationale: There was nothing one could have done for Glaube. Glaube acted in a tactically clumsy manner. He, Wilke, regretted the outcome. But could one really have foreseen the result?

District Court Judge Wilde

Hallmark: Listlessness, in many respects, even weakness. On the other hand, one has a right to one's weakness, it is one of the fundamental rights of the individual.

Snapshot: Wilde and his wife.

At the cafe. The wonderful fact that she looks at him, says tender things (even when Wilde doesn't know what to say) and sticks to the melody, like those competitors who hold their own against out-of-town celebrities and are applauded on the playing field: she always knows what else to say; the incredible fact that she is always capable of reacting, of moving her face in a new way, and as the fiasco still hasn't arrived, Wilde looks away. Then tries once again. And yet is unable to look at his wife for long without moving to the resting places to the right and left of her ears. She looks at his mouth, and, in his uncertainty, he begins to speak; she looks at him tenderly and he purses his lips.

Later, the magic hour is over. It becomes apparent that no progress has been made today. The sorceress lolls back in her seat as talk turns to leaving. The boredom of change. With no time left for sensible movements, he paws at her hair; she fends him off but doesn't laugh; instead, she clucks her tongue against the roof of her mouth and purses her lips like a housewife having choose between too many goods. He pays and she stands up ungracefully; he fetches her coat, listlessly; they have a long marriage ahead of them.

Wilde makes up for his listlessness in trial: he recently sent 12 prostitutes to the workhouse.

Participated against Glaube: As secretary of the disciplinary committee, he is obliged to participate in its meetings.

Rationale: In service, no consideration can be given to personal weaknesses. In this respect, his participation in the meeting did not allow any conclusions to be drawn about his attitude towards Glaube. On the other hand, this was not to say that he disapproved of the outcome.

District Court Judge L.

'Tuer avec cérémonies'

Hallmark:

Ordinance

I. Upon order of the court, Thadeusz Piatzowski—Cath.—is to be executed at 3 p.m.

II. Medical officers will be provided.

III. The corpse, if no further order is made, will be delivered to the Brandenburg police.

IV. For information and further reference Mr Reg. Med. councillor, priest, business inspector, chief constable's office.

L.

Ordinance

On Monday, 10 January 1944, at the local entity, the following executions were administered: SAO of the Court WK Berlin-Charlottenburg

1. former private Reinhard Zitter
2. former soldier Nikolaus Panzer
3. former infantryman Anthon

L.

Snapshot: Judge L. cannot stand it when defendants or convicts are unable to control themselves. Often people speak in the middle of the oral explanations for the verdict, or shout, or cry, although in such a state they are most certainly unable to follow the reasons for their sentences. In 1943, a condemned man who was to be placed on the guillotine prostrated himself unrestrainedly before the public prosecutor and the supervising judge, tucking his legs up against his body (as if suffering from appendicitis), so that he could not be stretched out even with the help of those present; they made every effort to bring the undignified kneeling man within the guillotine's reach. In another case, the wife of a condemned man, a young Polish woman, clung to Judge L. and clutched him in the groin, which was perceived as embarrassing by all those present.

Participated against Glaube: If Glaube committed a criminal offence against his adoptive daughter, then he also consented to her being punished.

Rationale: Sentencing is an art which begins with the establishment of facts. In this respect, the hearing before the disciplinary committee had failed. It was by no means clear that Glaube had committed an offence against P. Assuming, however, that Glaube *had* committed an offence against P., the fact that no punishment had taken place, only a form of self-punishment, was a flaw. It was doubtful whether Glaube's self-punishment satisfied the violation of the law. The entire handling of the case showed a failure on the part of the presiding judge, Korti.

Korti

I, Korti, was born 03.09.1909 in Flörsheim on the Main. I attended primary school and secondary school in S. I studied law in Marburg from the summer of 1929 until the summer of 1931; in autumn 1931, I passed the first state exam in law. I took the second state exam in Berlin in December 1935 after completing my legal training and attending National Socialist summer camp in Jüterbog. During the war, I took a leave of absence as a courts-martial councillor and reported to the front, as I'd realized that would get me transferred to Army Group von Blaskowitz in southern France. Otherwise, I would have had to continue signing courts-martial verdicts in Croatia. In 1942, I did not believe that the war would take an unfortunate turn, and even less that punishment would eventually be carried out by the German judiciary itself, as various colleagues of mine appear to be threatened with today; I did, however, fear acts of revenge by the partisans we were fighting, some of whose comrades I'd had to have executed. From the point of view of our leadership, I approved of these combat measures; at the same time, I preferred to withdraw from such duties. I had the opportunity to be transferred to France as an officer candidate, and I seized it. I think happily of my time in Croatia, a country where we were truly the conquerors, and wine and 'women' were for the taking. In France, on the contrary, strict discipline was the rule. On the other hand: Who doesn't like to be in France? I would say, however, that the greatest time of my life was in the Balkans, even if—in retrospect and for reasons of principle—I find it more correct that I did not over-extend my brief happiness there. Many of my friends from the artillery who stayed down there paid for those fulfilling years with their deaths, and I have never understood the connection between love and death, nor do I approve of it, in the same way that I don't like opera. I generally avoid extreme decisions. At any given moment, my view is made up of various circumstances, considerations, ideas, waiting and logic. I would say that there is almost something creative about it, because it involves a lot of experience. Here, too, the individual is a part of a large organization, in war an army group or a division, in peace a member of the administration of justice. I do not believe that it makes any practical difference if an individual nevertheless feels himself to be an independent spirit.

Today, I still find my decision to become a judge the right one. Though it's true that a judge makes less than an economist, every other occupation contains much greater risk. If a judge observes certain precautionary measures, he need not fear the state, his superiors nor politics, nor the churches or associations; he is an independent judge in the true sense of the word; the independent judge of the 1950s has succeeded the judge of the 1920s who belonged to the state. Hence, the bench is the most protected place in society (whereby, to avoid any misunderstandings, I would like to point out that I do not commit criminal offences and am therefore not at risk). Having said that, my experiences, especially during the Third Reich and the ensuing occupation, have taught me that our natural instinct for caution leads to better results than any other natural instinct.

Judges are in a different position today than they were 30 years ago. Appealing to the Grand Criminal Chamber is the only way to limit a judge's initiative. In 1943, for example, I had the opportunity to marry a noblewoman, a certain Fräulein von Zachwitz, not at all bad looking, indeed the bride's parents in Berlin were already well involved in wedding preparations when they received my cancellation telegram. Just knowing the possibility existed was enough for me, realizing it was unnecessary in practice. In the years of misery from 1945 to 1947, when the courts were not working or only to a limited extent, such a marriage would certainly have led to tensions. Besides, in 1943, I had other plans and wasn't interested in divorcing my wife, whom I had met in Croatia. Unfortunately, the black-market period and my desolate condition as a sickly returning-officer candidate without a judgeship cancelled out the authority I'd acquired in Croatia. My wife left me; she cheated on me with a businessman and left me when I tolerated it, although I'd thought I was keeping her by doing so. I admit that I did the wrong thing back then. I often long for my former wife, whose whereabouts I'm made aware of from cards as well as occasional visits, just as I fondly remember my time in Croatia and often long to return. On the other hand, life as a judge in the district of S. is satisfying. I will soon be the longest-serving judge when my colleagues Kaiser, Spetzel, Schwerin, Peitl, Wiesloch, Wirth and Albert pass away, which is to be expected. The post of senior magistrate will also soon be vacant, and I don't quite see how the president intends to pass me over for the new appointment, as I fulfil my duties punctually; I also believe, despite some disputes, that the president likes me. None of this is Croatia, mind you, but it is the best conceivable solution under the circumstances of the moment and the situation.

III
Korti in Private

Snow White

A few toilets are wrapped in paper like rosebushes and tied with cords. Korti tried to hit the pink urinal cakes.

He avoids the pub where he'd have to drink again and makes his way home. In Schmiedestraße, a large shop window has been smashed. A beautiful princess lies behind the riddled pane. Her cheap little purse hangs on her arm, her slim arm on a sliver of glass. Otherwise, all that is there is glass hanging from the top and sides of the frame—the arm with its vulnerable veins on the edge of the glass, but this does not affect the spell. But when Korti lifts up the arm with the handbag, a bloody cut appears on the underside. He manoeuvres the beautiful girl out of the shop window, where she is sleeping, drunk as a corpse, and lugs her to his flat on his back, a warm, soft burden that does not wake up. He lowers her down, which causes her to contort backwards, so he tips her sideways onto the floor where she remains sleeping. Then he puts her to bed, and, after eating something in the kitchen, thinks about playing the prince, but as he has too much beer in his bladder, he can't. She hasn't noticed anything and goes on sleeping in his pyjamas, only opening her eyes once to snuggle up to him before falling back asleep. Maybe he could be a prince after all, but he leaves things as they are.

Early in the morning, he makes her a coffee, as he wants to know what kind of voice she has. By the time he comes back from the kitchen, she is dressed and even has the shabby little bag in her hand, this is the way she probably wants to remain unrecognizable; unlike the little bag, the clothes that had been lying around were expensive and seductive. Not knowing why he's in such a hurry, Korti brings the woman to a pub he knows. He is startled when the pub landlord's cat, whom he knows inside and out, bumps him on the elbow. A cat with owl-like eyes, in the past that kind of cat was known as a black tree rider; sometimes, it is also claimed that the Mongolians are descended from wild cats. The lovely woman asks what frightened Korti so. She orders beers, intending to start the day off right with a nice morning pint, the lovely woman quite amenable: Yes. But Korti grows anxious, doesn't know where it all might lead. He excuses himself for a moment and goes to the toilet, where he finds a path that leads to freedom.

A Day in the Life of Korti

Korti regularly gets up at 7 a.m. and listens to the 'Frankfurter Wecker' on the radio. Breakfast is prepared. Earlier, during the war,

Korti had a wife, but she left him high and dry. After breakfast, Korti goes for a walk in the city park until 8.30. Around 9 a.m., he appears at work. There are days when there is little to do. Before 10, Korti shows up with the files from his desk that he has gone through and enquires after new ones. There are seldom any. The office manager keeps some things in reserve because he knows that Korti 'needs food' on days when there is little work; otherwise, he makes rationalization proposals for the office's work or drafts multi-purpose forms, of which there are already enough. This lack of anything to do does not apply to meeting days, however, when the day is completely full save a short break for the canteen. Korti schedules his appointments close together, thereby creating a work overload, a vortex that stimulates the strength to work, makes the brain more alert, heightens caution. He formulates better on such harvest days than on normal days, which is why, on those days, he dictates the reasons for his verdicts one after the other. A similar overload occurs on consultation days and when deputizing, which Korti, like every judge, is, to a certain extent, obliged to do. Midday in the canteen: the hot soup sharpens one's senses, invigorates the head and body, the most-of-the-time well-prepared main dish thereafter replenishes one's strength. (During negotiations, from 12 o'clock onwards, Korti is restless, he tends to get a little testy. At 12.30, he goes to eat. In summer, there is often a refreshing chilled soup and a soft compote that nestles on the palate, which Korti gobbles up quickly.) In the afternoon, there is often little to do. Korti has the new arrivals from the prison shown to him and visits the remand centre for the thousandth time. He does not fall for the unjustified complaints of some of the unruly prisoners. He knows the weaknesses of the prison staff; he can tell when a complaint is justified: he remedies it. Around 5 o'clock in autumn, it gets dusky in the wide corridors of the prison building. There is little public traffic. In winter, all the lights in the rooms of the public prosecutor's office and the district attorney's office are on at this time, and the judges have usually left. On his walk around the court building, Korti tries to work out whether the personnel savings made by working longer hours at the public prosecutor's office aren't offset by the waste of light during the night. Korti would like to have a company car and a driver. As a Court of Audit official, he would be suitable; Korti does not see any chances of becoming president of the Regional Court; he could become president of the Court of Audit. The president of the Court of Audit is entitled to a company car.

Korti leaves the building late, around 7 p.m. He is always available for Sunday duty, too. Once home, he turns the lights on low. He receives few guests. He can barely persuade his old girlfriends to spend the night in S. But then his bachelor apartment does just fine. As he remains cautious, visits are limited to girlfriends he had during the war, whom he met back when he was a soldier. He seldom accepts invitations to visit colleagues, evenings which usually consist of nibbling on pretzel sticks and being expected to drink sour Mosel wine. He goes to bed around midnight. This rhythm is of course disrupted when there is a lot of work to do. At those times, Korti goes to bed at 10, gets up at 6 a.m., doesn't have a second to spare for walks. A state of intoxication arises from the eagerness with which he devotes himself to the work that assails him, from the rush of hours and impressions, that he would not want to miss. In the past, it was believed that one developed into a human being in one's free time by cultivating the Self. As far as Korti is concerned, that process doesn't lead to a thing beyond nervousness, boredom, a feeling of abandonment. No, it was in that kind of work frenzy that Korti (his head filled with the rapid completion of tasks) gained direct access to people. At those moments, he could interview a witness or employee, take an interest in them and continue the conversation, even if 40 people were waiting outside. That's how Korti got to know his girlfriend, Reinhild K. This young woman who had fled Thuringia, with a hairstyle Korti was familiar with from Croatia (the kind that continued to exist only in the Eastern Bloc), made a statement before him, as the appointed judge, against her husband who had remained in Thuringia and from whom she wanted to be divorced. Without a second thought Korti paid her a visit that same evening. He would never have dared something like that during a period of normal activity.

An Offer to Become a Constitutional Judge in Mali

At the beginning of May, Korti receives an offer to become a constitutional judge in the recently independent Republic of Mali. His former superior, Dr R. in Hamburg, had recommended him. Korti could have transformed his post at the court in S. into a vacancy and accepted the offer without losing his entitlements to a pension in Germany. He began to inform himself about the climate in Mali. But due to the unstable global situation, he renounced that extra tour.

A Problem Comes Korti's Way

A 19-year-old automechanic killed his father, who dealt in scrap. Down on the street in front of the marital home at Luisenstr. 26, the father threateningly approached the car in which the family sat. That was the moment the son pulled the trigger.

Korti wanted to create a uniform atmosphere, a prerequisite for any verdict, in the session before the court of lay assessors: He tried to work out the boy's criminal disposition. But the representative of the youth-welfare office immediately raised objections. Later, Korti wanted to move towards an acquittal. It might have been possible to win over the lay assessors, but from the juvenile prosecutor's piqued attitude Korti sensed that there were also difficulties in that line of negotiation.

Korti lived in the hope that he could get rid of that particular case without having to give a verdict. After the meeting ended without results, he thought long and hard about how he could get rid of the case, how he could cause it to either fall apart or close it.

Another Problem That Comes Korti's Way

It had to do with a young girl, S., from a refugee family in a village at the edge of the judicial district. The locals avoided the family. Within the family there was a case of incest. The girl accused a villager of having abused her. The police believed S.'s brother-in-law to be the perpetrator. Later, the girl's older brother was considered the primary suspect. When suspicion fell on the girl's father, who worked away from home, the girl asked the interrogating detective: Who knows about this? So far, only me, the detective replied. When he took the defendant back to the room where she was being temporarily detained and turned his back on her to unlock a door, she grabbed his neck and squeezed with her—too small—finger bones. All in all, a difficult case. Korti gave her a two-year rehabilitative sentence. Following the verdict, Korti and the detective were sitting in the canteen. They figured that S. would go looking for her father as soon as she was released from prison. If she didn't find him at her former place of employment, she'd probably keep looking for him until she did. If he'd already been released from prison, that is!

Approach to Solving the Problem

Why, when your father was lying on the pavement and bleeding but still moaning, in other words, not yet dead, did you squat next to him and fire a second shot at him? This is the question Korti asked to open the second juvenile-court session against the 19-year-old mechanic who had shot his father.

And what were you doing until you went to the phone box and called the police? What did you discuss with your mother and your girlfriend, who tried to snatch the gun from you before you shot your father, who was coming towards the car, or rather—let me correct myself—before you hit your shot father on the head with the butt of the gun, fracturing his skull? Korti carefully considered every detail of the crime in the hope of finding a solution. He read the files and asked questions. An acquittal seemed too sensational to him, a rehabilative sentence had to be well chosen and not appear ridiculous, for a juvenile sentence the mood had to be sounded out and prepared first.

The Sleeper Hoping for One to Come

At a carnival event, Korti did not take part in the restless hustle and bustle of the many couples, but lay down on a daybed instead, the event was taking place in private rooms, from his place outside the action he watched the dancers and even managed to sleep for a while, thus keeping himself fresh to maybe become active again later. He really hoped someone would come and sit down next to him; many couples wondered about the sleeper, who did not leave his resting place until the end of the party and was so tired that he had to be driven home.

Laurel-Leaf Adventure

The bar was set up in a way that forced you to walk up a set of stairs and then squat down: a children's floor where you couldn't stand up straight but couldn't be seen either. Korti felt defeated in his new shirt, which upset the balance of heat in his body, those tight trousers belted around his belly, possibly cutting off his blood flow. What use was the favourable opportunity that he had her sitting in front of him in this children's paradise? He couldn't come up with any opening. He watched the one he'd been following for a long time now: how her silver-painted nails, writing, turned the table into a place of unrest, cigarette holder, gorges in the skin around her chin; warts along the temples, on her hand a signet ring like a wart, fringe-covered forehead, eyes hooded in heavy green and silver makeup; sprigs of laurel on her dress, a winner with fingernails of silver.

After a little while, Korti's shirt was so damp with sweat from simply watching that he had to go home and change. Before that, however, he had to settle the horrendous bill for a glass of whiskey; they made you pay dearly for that kind of return trip to childhood in the bar; on the other hand, they only saved on materials by building on a smaller scale. What one was paying for was the rarity of such a place and that forbidden return to childhood standards. By the time Korti returned in fresh shirt and trousers, certain of victory this time, the woman he'd been admiring for so long from afar—an actress, he assumed—had left.

Removal and Subsequent Meal

Many judges at the time adored, indeed were in love with, the young chamber singer S., who was conducting a major tenancy case before the district court and therefore could often be seen in the building. Like many colleagues, Korti sent her flowers. After doing this for some time, one evening he asked her to go out with him. He'd called the theatre manager's office and found out that she had no commitments that particular day at the opera house. He was turned down. In the evening, however, a group of people turned up at his door wanting to take him to a duck dinner. The beautiful singer was not among them, but she'd told friends that Councillor Korti was alone and at home. The roast duck was served in a hunting lodge prepared for receptions. For Korti, the meal, which was accompanied by champagne, made up for everything. Ladies were also present, but Korti was unable to sit near any of them. Instead, he was allowed to chat to a business manager. There is a surrogate for everything.

Reminiscence

A young woman ordered two vol-au-vents, torte and ice cream, and, while waiting for them, pet her dog. Korti immediately thought of Maria, his lost wife.

A More Exact Reminiscence

Was there any chance of reunion when Frau Maria Korti visited her husband Korti one weekend in 1956? Or was it just a whim that had come over her? Korti drank a rather large amount of alcohol that night, he was completely surprised by her arrival. On the one hand, he was fearful of losing his bachelor's life; on the other, he didn't want to let her out of his sight for even a second, as she sat on the barstool next to him with her brown lama eyes and told him things she thought would please him. He could not free himself from the prison of his routines, grew tired by around 10 o'clock; nothing in common with the good old days in Croatia. In the hopes of nevertheless harnessing the unexpected, Korti promised a golden future, a new Korti. To everything, Maria responded: Yes.

How Was Maria's Yes to Be Understood?

She didn't even consider whether she wanted what Korti was promising, as that would have complicated things. From his words she gathered that he wanted her around again, and so she prolonged the feeling that she'd found protection with him by listening to him and agreeing to all his plans. She said *yes* without reservation, because she reckoned that these things, i.e. Korti's changes, simply would not happen, that he'd be back to his old self the very next week. In her life, she would only have made firm promises for things she knew would not happen. If she was determined that something was unlikely to happen, she could promise, but she would have been too superstitious to make a promise for something she truly wished for herself. But she was no longer sure that she wished to stay with Korti.

Bad Luck and Organization

Later, after Maria had left him, and a little after she had handed him the divorce papers, Korti thought that maybe she hadn't liked his bachelor's flat. He moved out and into a completely new place, reorganized all his habits in the hope that, that way, perhaps he'd be ready for a second return of his wife. That was the time the case-assignment plan was redone; Korti was swamped by work. He was put in charge of the court library. Expected to preside over the jury court. Money had to be transferred. A new budget for the judicial district of S. had to be arranged and the office reorganized. Korti experiences disappointment and rejection in his private life, and yet there is also a system of protection against private misfortune that has transformed every misfortune which has affected him into organization. Korti is invulnerable.

IV
Korti's End?

Sum Total

From which side do they still hope to harm Korti? He is protected in front by the independence of the judiciary. Korti does not make any mistakes that could cost him such independence. His flanks are protected by his fellow judges. Behind him are the German people, whom he represents with his sentences. The Grand Criminal Chambers cannot dismiss him, his superiors cannot instruct him. Not even Hitler was able to conquer the judiciary. Korti sits firmly within the spider's web of justice. Who can conquer Korti? No one who is unable to conquer the judiciary first.

An Abbreviated Course on the German Justice System

Barbaric Justice Following the Year 1300

Following the year 1300, the judiciary emerged in response to the rapid rise in crime in the fourteenth century. The judiciary took its resources from crime. When these means were directed not only against highwaymen, arsonists and coin counterfeiters, but also against suspicious citizens. After the year 1400, protection was also sought against the judiciary. The forms of justice provided protection against the judiciary.

Superficial Romanization after 1400

The judiciary's forms were taken from Roman legal history. Below the forms, the justice system remained as it was. Thus, it was divided into civil law, criminal law and law enforcement: a rational superstructure, a Christian-medieval middle structure and a barbaric substructure. Later, no one dared cut up the mature, fifteenth-century centaur body.

Love for Justice (amor juris)

This judiciary was never intended to serve justice. After 1300 and 1400, no one intended to introduce justice. Thus, though the judiciary defends the idea of justice against an unjust world within its walls, justice itself never lived there. Cut off from its supply areas in the idea, the judiciary becomes perverse. It protects, as it protects against many other things, against justice. And so, who loves the judiciary? All those who have to fear change.

Rationalism without Enlightenment

In the eighteenth century, the judiciary was also subject to the Enlightenment. The Enlightenment in Germany after 1700 did not enlighten per se; on the contrary, it took steps to enlighten within the framework of what existed. In the judiciary there were: (1) the judges' personal views; (2) the judges' superiority over the accused; (3) legal scholarship, which kept the basis of new talent narrow and did not endanger the profession with too many new recruits; (4) a special class of jurists on their way to becoming professional civil servants; (5) logic's sharp sword and the tools of the executioner. From these components, a precisely functioning judicial machine emerged. A justice system, however, that developed its strength from the dangers that threatened it.

Fredrick II and the Justice System

In the eighteenth century, the judiciary found itself under great threat in the form of Frederick II of Prussia, transferred to a barbaric country as king, who at least attempted to reform the justice system. As soon as he came to power, he banned burning-at-the-stake and torture. The judiciary made itself very small. Frederick's first Grand Chancellor for Justice was a Koch (1747–55). The second, von Jarriges, was a nobleman once again (1755–70). The third, Karl Joseph Max Baron von Fürst und Kupferberg, was of high nobility and no longer received commoners (1770–79). When, after long wars, the king sensed he did not have much time left but was still far from having asserted himself against the judiciary (rather, the old-style judiciary was beginning to spread again), he provoked a scandal: the Miller Arnold case. As a shock measure, several judges and government lawyers were sent to Spandau Fortress, and Grand Chancellor von Fürst und Kupferberg was dismissed. The judiciary learnt to protect itself during those years. Justice was restored immediately after the king's death. The king died in the spring of 1786, and, in the autumn of 1786, Berlin once again presented the spectacle of a human burning.

Out of the crisis emerged a legal profession with renewed self-confidence, strengthened by the addition of the profession of cameralists and auditors. Later crises—after 1920, after 1933 and after 1945—no longer affected the judiciary. The school of the past 660 years, but especially the school of the eighteenth century, has made the judiciary hard. It has developed a method of thinking in which common sense and logic, logic and general concepts, general concepts and common sense support each other. It has developed exact methods. Exact methods can hardly be shaken off again. The judicial system is resistant to external attack. The future belongs to such an institution.

Towards Everlasting Peace from Out of the Spirit of Justice

The end of the world, Max Frisch says, has become enforceable. It can therefore be assumed that, in the future, the nations of the world governed by the rule of law will switch to solving their difficulties using the methods of justice. Then there will be no more changes. The judiciary in all countries is preparing for this future task. The focus is on training the next generation.

Practice Cases for Judiciaries-to-Be

33. A widow who remarries has brought a wine shop or a furniture shop into the marriage. Can the husband (in the statutory matrimonial property regime) lawfully sell the wines and furniture in stock to third parties (Gb. 1376/1)?

48. As a result of caterpillar damage, it becomes necessary to cut down a forest in the marital usufruct (Gb. 1363). If the husband goes bankrupt, can the wife claim the felled wood from the estate?

52. A. notices a treasure in a stream. B. whistles to his dog to take it. C. takes the treasure from out of the dog's mouth. To whom does the treasure belong?

85. If, due to dipsomania, Falstaff had become incapacitated, what would he have owed the pub landlady where, without the consent of his guardian, he had consumed more than 8 schillings worth of Sekt and ½ penny's worth of bread?

150. Hoping to be promoted, a first lieutenant, immediately before the captain, has bought a horse; the seller, however, takes advantage of an opportunity to sell the horse to a sportsman at a better price. Can the officer, who has now been promoted, demand the horse back from the sportsman to whom it has been handed over?

194. In the absence of her husband, a wife sells his dog, which she does not like, for 100 marks. She tells her husband it's run away. Suddenly the dog reappears, and now the man to whom she'd sold it to sells it to another man for 80 marks. But as the first buyer comes forward, the husband learns the true facts and now authorizes the more advantageous first purchase. Can the first buyer demand the dog from the second? If the man had pledged the returned dog to a forester who had given him a loan, would the lien remain in force after the sale authorized by the woman? Even if the forester knew of the unauthorized sale by the wife at the time of the pledge?

197. On Wednesday, 13 June 1930, at 10 a.m., someone promised to pay a debt within 8 days (or 14 days, 4 weeks, 1 month, 1 year, etc.). When did the deadline expire?

228. A disabled man attempts to kiss a girl. Unable to resist him otherwise, she pushes him into the stream flowing by the side of the road, causing him to develop a prolonged illness due to the cold he catches from falling into the water. Must she reimburse his care?

275. A traveller has stolen a box of cigars from another person in steerage and gradually smoked them all. If the steamer sinks shortly afterwards, and the one whose things have been stolen disappears without a trace along with all their effects, does this release the thief—who was rescued—from the obligation to replace the value of the cigars?

287. In Karl Immermann's novel *Münchhausen*, the alleged sword of Charlemagne is stolen from a court schoolmaster out of spite. Sued for damages, could the thief demand the transfer of the court schoolmaster's ownership claims?

310. There is a lawyers' conference in X. District Judge A. there writes to his friend, Assessor B., to offer him a room. B. happily accepts. Is the contract binding? If A.'s maid tears a hole in B.'s trousers while cleaning his clothes, is A. liable for damages?

321. A dog owner intending to go on a summer holiday makes a deal with a forester who will—for a fixed fee—take care of his dog during the month of August. At the end of July, the dog bites a child and, angry about the resulting costs, his master has him killed. Does he nevertheless have to pay the forester the agreed sum?

448. Intending to get married, as compensation someone gives a woman with whom he'd had a relationship a debt certificate worth over 1,000 marks. Is the debt certificate valid?

455. A widow has a house in Nießbrauch. In return for payment, she authorizes another party to exercise this usufructuary right. When she terminates based on Law 565, the other party claims that 595 is instead decisive, as rights can only be leased, not rented.

682a. A headmaster has paid his traveller a month's salary in advance at the latter's request. The traveller gambles it away and shoots himself. Are his heirs liable for repayment?

700. An incapacitated mentally ill man handed over securities belonging to him to a banker for sale, immediately received 3,000 marks but did not collect the remaining amount. A few days later, he is found dead without the 3,000 marks. If the banker has made 11,000 marks from the securities, does he owe the mentally ill man's heirs 11,000 marks, or only 8,000?

702. At Christmas, a student's aunt anonymously sends him a bottle of liquor, which, by mistake, is given to his roommate of the same name. If the latter drinks the bottle, does the aunt or the other student have any claim against him? Does it depend on the *bona* or *mala fides* of the recipient?

701a. Can the church owner who restored the church set on fire by X. demand compensation for his expenses from X.?

Korti's Dream

A massive elephant body, like a crane, whose profitability is doubtful. Moving one step back, the elephant crushes the employee who was handling something at its back. For a long time, the giant mass stands motionless. Then it begins to take an interest in the employee's body. It does a headstand, which is part of its act, on the employee's chest. In a headstand and therefore rather harmless, the murderer could simply have been shot. It would have been possible to reach the weak points on the head, especially the ears, which were marked with white chalk lines. But because such an elephant—a huge, very nervous African elephant, which is quite a feat to train—is of great value, the people involved refrained from doing so.

Korti's Monologue

Perhaps this beautiful autumn means we don't have much longer to live. The spring of 1945 was particularly beautiful, too. Nevertheless, most people survived. So we can hope we will survive this autumn as well—assuming it really is as dangerous as they say. I read in a paper that you can donate your sperm to a sperm bank; in the case of a catastrophe, there will be enough reproductive material. This was the autumn of 1961, marvelled at by all meteorologists, and which, despite its beauty, paleness and length, was not followed by any kind of catastrophe.

The Hall of Justice Fire of 1943/44

That tragic New Year's Eve terrorist attack of 1943 which set the old hall of justice on Schwarzenbergplatz ablaze also signalled the end of a generation of judges. This is not to say that even one judge was burnt to death, but the traditional sense of continuity that had existed since 1713 for every judge—apart from a few outsiders—in the old court building did not return after the war. At that time, President Mangold was still alive. As soon as he became aware of the fire, he went to the site with the gentlemen of the regional court and the district-court directors. The fire brigades, directed to the suburbs with advance warning, i.e. before the attack, had survived the attack unscathed and worked their way along the partially buried streets to the centre of the city. Some assessors and councillors had appeared in front of the district court; the old district court, opposite the district court, still appeared intact, but was later demolished by a time-delay bomb that had been overlooked in the roof truss. A fire chief who appeared at the scene said the district court was irretrievably lost. The president, however, did not want to give up the valuable building without a fight. Together with some councillors, he went to the upper floors and tried to resolve the situation. With his councillors, companions, party members and office staff who were now arriving, he formed a chain through which flammable material was brought down to the street from the top floors. Afterwards, at least the land registers were saved. A final personal effort helped to save the land registers.

The Court Could Reopen in Autumn 1945

On the night of the fire in which the hall of justice burnt all the way down to its cellar, district-court councillors tossed crucifixes and benches out of the upper-floor windows. Mountains of files arose in the courtyard. Which were partially stored in incorrect fashion by Hitler Youth. In autumn 1945, the new building, which had been taken over following the dissolution of the Wehrmacht, was 'open for business' once again.

Inspector Hansheinz Naleppa Reports

As soon as the all-clear was given, we in the office were sent by messenger to the district court. I have to say that, as a member of the judiciary, I would have gone to the Palace of Justice immediately anyway. The attic of the district court was ablaze, you could see that as soon as you approached. I saw the President, the District Court councillors Erbe, Dr Friedrich, Dr Heintze, Wiegand. Some district-court councillors searched the district court, which had remained intact and was later shaken by an explosion that killed Councillor Schmidt. The next day we all went to the funeral. I must mention that President Mangold was already in the district-court building with some gentlemen when we arrived. He was always the first on duty, despite his injuries from the First World War, and thus was a living example of what he'd always told us: we on the front line of the judiciary were fighting on behalf of the great change in the fate of the people. When Hegel, whom I read from time to time in my spare time—whereas I dislike Schopenhauer and Nietzsche for their obscurity—speaks of the life of the idea in reality, I think about applying this practically to justice, which is to a certain extent both idea and reality insofar as it embodies the daily struggle that took place at the same time on both the Eastern and air front during which numerous office staff were killed. There is a plaque about it in the corridor of the new court building (the former military district command). For us, President Mangold's intervention was another sign that the idea was directly linked to reality. There was little hope of saving the upper floors. We watched—while on duty ourselves—the district-court judges throw crucifixes and benches out of the upper-floor windows. Mountains of files in the courtyard. Some of them had been improperly stored by Hitler Youth. An empty zone was supposed to stop the fire between the third and second floors, but this hope remained unrealized. That night, the building burnt all the way down to the cellar. For many of us, it was the end of an era, as soon afterwards we were moved into new buildings, first municipal ones, and then in 1946, under the new president, into the military district command, built by leading architects in 1935. President Mangold very quickly realized that it was impossible to save the old district court. So our efforts were focussed on saving the land registers and the tables, some of which were quite valuable, and the equally valuable benches, some of which had been carved in the eighteenth century. The library could not be saved. The president did not outlive the fire by much. We all went to his funeral in March 1944 and the court staff were given the day off. As a result, this universally popular, albeit strict, president did not have to live to see his friend Dr Kranzler become involved in the 20 July plot shortly thereafter. We in the office have never been able to get used to another president or a new building; naturally, this does not apply to the new members of the office. I have to say that the fire was like a caesura. A judiciary that no one could force to back down, to which even King Frederick II of Prussia tipped his hat, had to give up floor by floor, room by room in a tenacious struggle. Much of the documentation was lost, and it's quite possible that not just a few defendants were able to survive 1945 without facing any criminal proceedings. The judges who survived this fire were never able to regain their old self-confidence, which was based on the existence of the intact building, just as it is certainly not the same for a pastor when he preaches in a new building.

Inspector Berger Reports on the Einsatzgruppen Trial

As the president's personnel officer for many years—the personnel officer has full access to the files, I have only recently been replaced by Inspector Kaiser due to some misunderstandings, i.e. I am on leave until the conclusion of my disciplinary proceedings—I can provide information on the filling of the judges' posts in the judicial district of S.

There are several officers among our judges, by contrast, a very small number of former party members. This remarkable result sets us apart from other districts. Officers: Colonel Schwerin, Major Peitl, Captain Kaiser (holder of the Knight's Cross); military-court counsels: Stumpf, Kantorowicz, Dr Leipzig, Arnold, Wiesloch. 'Special court' judges in Poland: Bremser, Peickert, Hoffmann. Commissariat: Dr Wegeleben, Dr Beier, Dr Karsten. Navy: Höhne, Sauerbrey. The rest of the judges are either new or did not have any particular competences during the war. In addition: Korti,

Dr Glaube, Meinecke, Jakob, Dr Schwiethelm, Wiegand and the president. In addition: four women judges employed in the guardianship department. I admit that the way in which I obtained important documents may not always have been acceptable. In this context, however, I would like to emphasize that I have not collected any material on judges within our district. Having said that, the idea of having various presidents of the higher district courts and high-ranking judges of northern Germany testify in the Einsatzgruppen trial in Ulm—in their capacity as former Army Group judges—was based on a letter I wrote to various illustrated newspapers which was then taken up by the court in the trial. It made quite an important impression on us personnel officers that these high-ranking judges and presidents did not have to give statements under oath. The only reason could be that the court did not believe them. We were curious to see what kind of reception the judges, returning from their testimony, would get in their hometowns. I even expected one or other to be arrested and wrote another letter to the *Bild* to that effect, but our high expectations were disappointed.

Recovery of Judicial Self-Consciousness following the Einsatzgruppen Trial in Ulm

In the Einsatzgruppen trial in Ulm, various high-ranking judges were heard as witnesses in their capacity as former Army Group judges on the activities of the Einsatzgruppen commandos. These high-ranking judges and presidents gave statements but were not under oath and this remained the case after their testimony. The arrest of or disciplinary charge against one or other witnesses seemed inevitable. When almost nothing happened, it took a while, but eventually judicial self-confidence recovered.

An Excess of Severity in the 'Special Courts' in Poland

For some time, it seemed that the quota of executions following the Poland Special Criminal Law Regulation as well as the severity of penalties between 1942 and 1944 in Poland were generally too high. The newspapers suspected the judges' personal culpability. Nevertheless, in judicial district S., none of those judges who had been involved in the so-called special courts in Poland—this primarily concerned judges Bremser, Peickert and Hoffmann—were found guilty of wrongful acts.

A Conspiracy Is Uncovered

In winter 1959–60, various judges in S. began lightly increasing the severity of their sentences. Public prosecutors were instructed by Chief Public Prosecutor B. to appeal all sentences of less than one year in prison. Thus, lenient judges were punished for their leniency, as, for the most part, they drafted judgements for the court of appeals, in other words: they had to apply a double measure of care to the reasons for their verdicts. By the summer of 1960, the average sentence had increased by 30 to 40 per cent. In the prisons, the practice of pardoning was choked. Rather late, in the autumn of 1960, the president and the two presidents of the Grand Criminal Chambers were surprised to learn of the sentences being handed down in various individual cases and discovered what had been happening. The president as well as the presidents of the Grand Criminal Chambers did their best to reduce sentences again. This led to a great number of appeals on the part of defence lawyers in the winter of 1961, with the result that Trial Chambers I and II became hopelessly overloaded. Restoring the old level was impossible; the sentences remained, on average, 20 to 30 per cent higher. Those who suffered the damage sat in their cells. Nothing happened to the conspirators.

The Streetwalker as Lay Judge

In September 1959, the judicial administration in S. made a dreadful mistake, one, however, that was able to be rectified immediately. A certain Frau F., registered as a housewife in the civil register of the municipality of G., was drawn by lot as a lay judge and assigned to the Juvenile Court of Lay Assessors for the letters A to K. It later came to light that the woman had been engaged in prostitution. She was immediately punished for false declaration of marital status. The sentences in which she had participated were, of course, overturned on appeal.

Korti and the Death Penalty

Experience has shown that judges are held accountable for death sentences later on, especially during critical times when death sentences become more frequent. Political opinion soon changes and the judge who pronounced the death sentence is left without cover and must justify their behaviour. For this reason, Korti believed that the judiciary should not wade anywhere near the dangerous waters of the death sentence, even if it certainly contributed to many of the judges' public reputation and personal pride, even if the decision of life and death lay in their hands.

Korti's Favourite Dish

Korti's favourite dish is lentils. Christmas Eve: carp *au bleu*. New Year's Eve: sandwiches. Easter: lamb.

Korti, Endless

Korti's adventurous journey to the end, which is already lurking somewhere, is accompanied by good intentions. Of late, these good intentions include the renunciation of curiosity regarding traffic.

In the spring of 1961, Korti was almost run over by a motor vehicle as he curiously approached the site of an accident surrounded by rubberneckers. In the ensuing fall, he broke both his lower legs. The doctors restored Korti's ability to function. Now Korti's sense of caution extends to this type of misfortune in particular. Indeed, there is little misfortune in the world to which Korti's caution does not extend. And yet, he remains apprehensive: this apprehension, however, is also a source of strength. The judges in the district of S., but the judiciary elsewhere, too, are cooperating on a security system that—while renouncing many forms of activity—will prolong Korti's end as well as that of others. Around 1800, a newspaper article would have been enough to depose Korti; around 1900, a reform movement would have been necessary, in 1962, not even a riot might be enough. And who on earth would start a riot over Korti? And so, Korti's end is still a long way off, indeed. At the moment, Korti's end is receding farther and farther into the distance.